Praise for Francis Levy's *EROTOMANIA: A ROMANCE*

★ *Queerty.com* Top 10 Book of 2008.
★ *Inland Empire Weekly* Standout Book of 2008.

"Levy is our generation's D.H. Lawrence, Henry Miller, and Charles Bukowski rolled into one."
—INLAND EMPIRE WEEKLY

"[*Erotomania*] is a great book, written with flawless verve by a tremendous fictioneer and thinker, and it deserves glory. A classic."
—ANDREI CODRESCU

"Levy seems to have an eye for detail for all that is absurd, commonly human, and uniquely American."
—BOOKSLUT

"Sex is familiar, but it's perennial, and Levy makes it fresh."
—LOS ANGELES TIMES

"The book's raw but thoughtful carnality comes off as at once serious, clever and crude in sending up the absurdities of contemporary hookings-up. It's not a traditional love story, but debut novelist Levy puts thought and genuine feeling behind all the doings."
—PUBLISHERS WEEKLY

"[*Erotomania*] can just as easily be a bookend to the beautifully nuanced prose of Milan Kundera as it can be a long-version story for a nudie mag minus the accompanying photographs. It's all in the context—as it is with most relationships."
—THE QUARTERLY CONVERSATION

"*Erotomania* wields a comedic punch that makes it, above all, a fun novel to read."
—NERVE

"A high-minded yet slapstick take on erotic d(
—TIME OUT CHICAGO

D1570615

SEVEN DAYS

a novel by

FRANCIS LEVY

in RIO

TWO DOLLAR RADIO
Books too loud to ignore

TWO DOLLAR RADIO is a family-run outfit founded in 2005 with the mission to reaffirm the cultural and artistic spirit of the publishing industry.

We aim to do this by presenting bold works of literary merit, each book, individually and collectively, providing a sonic progression that we believe to be too loud to ignore.

Copyright © 2011 by Francis Levy.
All rights reserved.
ISBN: 978-0-9826848-7-0
Library of Congress Control Number: 2011925180
Cover: Schiele, Egon. *Self Portrait with Chinese Lantern Plant.* 1912.
Author photograph by Hallie Cohen.

No portion of this book may be copied or reproduced, with the exception of quotes used in critical essays and reviews, without the written permission of the publisher.
This is a work of fiction. All names, characters, places, and incidents are products of the author's lively imagination. Any resemblance to real events or persons, living or dead, is entirely coincidental.

TWO DOLLAR RADIO
Books too loud to ignore
www.TwoDollarRadio.com
twodollar@TwoDollarRadio.com

RObO12 91Obb

For Titus, Zeno and Hallie.
I never thought group therapy would lead to this.

SEVEN DAYS

a novel by

FRANCIS LEVY

in RIO

AUTHOR NOTE

None of the characters in this novel are real, nor are the places or psychoanalytic movements, even though the name Rio may conjure the real city of Rio de Janeiro. Lacanian analysis as described in the novel bears no resemblance to the branch of psychoanalytic practice initiated by the French analyst Jacques Lacan. Even the duration of time stated in the title bears little resemblance to what is commonly known as seven days. So don't start writing irate letters to my blog correcting this or that or asking for refunds.

I went down to the Copacabana on my first night in Rio. I was told that most of the women were prostitutes who would gladly sleep with me for a hundred American dollars. I saw a sexy woman wearing high heels and an abbreviated bikini and decided that there was no sense in hesitating, since from what I'd heard about the lovemaking habits of Brazilians, one would be as talented as the next. I pursed my lips and made purring sounds like a pussycat to get the idea across, but the woman didn't seem to notice me, even though I was wearing a seersucker suit from the Brooks Brothers 1818 Collection. There aren't too many men wearing Brooks Brothers suits (or any suits for that matter) down by the Copacabana, and I would have thought I stood out from the crowd.

I have always found communication between myself and other human beings to be a problem, and often worry that I haven't succeeded with women where I otherwise might because my words get caught between my teeth. So I just held out my hand to her as she waited for the traffic light to change. "I'm Kenny," I said. "Do you understand *anglais*? I am new to your country and I wanted to introduce myself while also initiating myself into your highly permissive sexual culture. I will put my cards on the table: I'd be glad to engage you to perform sexual acts on me for a fee."

I don't speak a word of Portuguese, so for a moment I entertained the idea of simply squeezing her breasts and spanking her very ample and exposed buttocks. But common sense prevailed. I intuitively knew that it wasn't a good idea to touch the merchandise until we had worked out our fiduciary arrangement.

Even as she walked away from me I was convinced that if I had been more outspoken or demonstrative we might be on our way to a hotel room. *Fuck*, for instance, is one of those words that crosses cultural and class boundaries. I have said "fuck you" in hundreds of cities around the world, and everyone seems to know what I mean. Whether you're in Bangkok's famed Soi Cowboy, San Francisco's Tenderloin, Paris's Bois de Boulogne, Hamburg's Reeperbahn, or Amsterdam's Rossebuurt, *fuck* is as easily understood as the skull and bones. *Fuck* can be an expression of disgust or of longing. I should have simply asked, "Do you want to fuck?" and then we could have dealt with the logistics.

I had checked into my hotel room at the Copacabana only a few hours earlier. Both the young ladies at the reservations desk were absolutely astonishing. In fact, with their shiny, dark hair pulled tightly back and their ample cleavage adding just the right contrast to the formality of their blue uniforms, I could barely tell one from the other—though I did take note of a nameplate reading "Suzanne" on one of them, pledging to myself that by the end of my stay I would get up enough courage to offer her remuneration for her body. Upon arrival in Brazil, I immediately wanted to have sex with everyone, and by now I was already feeling nostalgic for that first flush of Brazilian pulchritude. I had carefully read the sex blogs, which described the easy familiarity of Brazilian women and the murky line that exists between prostitution and ordinary human interchanges.

I refused to allow the sting of my first encounter to deter me, so I lit off for an establishment called Café Brazil, which I had noticed when I drove up to the hotel. What better place to get into the spirit of a country than a bar named after it? Later on, I told myself, I would seek out the more exotic spots, like Café

Erotique. For all I knew, there might be a Café Whore, perhaps even a Café Nympho.

I had heard that although Rio was a paradise teeming with available women, you did have to look out for pickpockets and petty criminals. There were even some rumors about kidnappings by gangs of sexy women who titillated you even as they held you for ransom. But I hadn't reckoned with the simpler notion of being overcharged. In the great European capitals, American tourists are routinely handed menus with higher prices than what the locals pay. It was only after I had left Café Brazil, having made several clumsy and abortive attempts to wrangle a female escort, that I realized I had paid over $5 for my Diet Coke.

Returning to the hotel empty handed, I decided that it might be easier to simply go to the concierge desk and ask for sex. Come to think of it, it was probably included in my package deal.

"*Sim, Senhor* Cantor, I can arrange your girl," the concierge said after I very un-surreptitiously placed a pile of *reals* in his hand. "And what kind of girl are you looking for?"

"I want a sexy girl. Can you make sure she's sexy? I want someone with all the best features." It reminded me of the way my mother ordered fish over the phone: "I want a nice big piece of salmon, not too fatty."

I congratulated myself on my resourcefulness and headed back to my room to prepare for my first encounter with a Rio whore. I was so overwrought with anticipation that I practically jumped out of my shoes when I heard her knock on my door. She was darkly beautiful, with hair that hung almost to her waist, wearing a tight red cocktail dress. But she was like a New York City cab driver, chattering on her cell phone even as she lifted her skirt to show me her goods, whispering that she wanted the equivalent of $100. It felt so much like being in a New York cab that I accidentally blurted out "Forty-third and Fifth!" instead of telling her to dance a sexy merengue in the nude. As it turned out, this activity was not on the menu that she had handed me, with its numbered items printed in English and Portuguese. It was a rumpled sheet of paper that was divided into two columns, "Subversive" and "Dominican." The items under the "Subversive" heading were "shrimping," "rimming," "bandage," and "spanky." The "Dominican" list was more traditional, and included "fuck," "blowjob," "sixty-nine," "around the world," "half and half," and "caning"—this last item seeming rather anomalous and harsh.

I had a beautiful room that overlooked two ten-ton air conditioning units, whose vibration I could feel when I tried to pry open one of the sealed windows to let in some fresh air. I didn't want to lose the Carnival-like mood that was beginning to infect me, even if I had my doubts about the prospect of making love to somebody who was on the telephone. She was talking loudly and animatedly, all while trying to demonstrate her lovely private parts, and seemed like the kind of person who was perfectly capable of doing two things at once. I gave her a handful of *reals*.

"Look, Tiffany," I said, using my pet name for prostitutes, which I'd always thought should be mandated by the UN as an identifier in travel documents for international sex workers. "You're a gorgeous, wonderful, and special woman. I wanted to pay you a little extra for taking the trouble to perform your services while multi-tasking. But instead, I'm just going to pay you a kill fee so you can get on with your conversation and I can form a more focused relationship with another *puta*." I surprised even myself with this about-face, but Tiffany didn't seem to miss a beat. She continued with her conversation in rapid-fire Portuguese, picked up her things, and walked out as if she had rejected me and not the other way around.

Night was falling and there was an ambitious selection of adult films on pay-per-view. But I was in the sex capital of the world and I didn't want to resort to experiencing Brazilian life vicariously—at least not yet. I realized that Rio had a rich cultural history and that there were other things to do besides look for prostitutes, but I knew in my heart that I was only interested in sex.

There were probably as many Tiffanys on the beach outside the Copacabana as there were rats in the New York subway system. I just had to locate one who didn't insist on being plugged into a headset while she was administering fellatio. As I came to the bank of elevators on my floor, I noticed two middle-aged women who I assumed were retired prostitutes. I had imagined that aging whores retired to other cities like São Paulo, which is noted for its efficient mass transit system, so I was sure they were back in Rio for some recreational sex. Their skin was lined and leathery and they looked like they had been ravaged by age, but now they could use what was left of their looks to enjoy sex without having to worry about where the next *real* was coming from.

Since they were plainly over the hill, I thought they might be able to offer an objective view about where the best hookers could be found in Rio. I was sure they could give me a few tips on how to enjoy the rest of my stay. "Excuse me, ladies, my name is Kenny Cantor and I'm a tourist from Manhattan."

"Ah, Manhattan," they both sighed with deep Brazilian accents.

"I take it you are natives of Rio, real Brazilians. Carnival, the Copacabana…"

"Carnival is funny," the shorter one said. "Samba!" She started to dance with me, pushing me toward the elevator door just as it was opening, so that I lost my balance and almost careened into several hookers who were already in the elevator. The old whores were still laughing as the door shut without our even having had a chance to say goodbye.

I could have propositioned the girls coming down from their assignations, but I employ the same attitude toward prostitutes that I do toward baked goods—*get 'em while they're hot*. I had wanted to get to know the two old pros because I was sure they could tell me where all the fresh, young women congregated, where the supply was greater than the demand. I wanted to start my visit with a woman who hadn't become jaded and stale from overuse. I sincerely hoped that my first experience had been an anomaly and that the prostitutes of Rio were not like New York cabbies, constantly speaking to people in other countries.

With the advent of the Blackberry and the iPhone, it was going to become very difficult to find prostitutes who were free of the multi-tasking that had become a fixture of modern life. The old-fashioned streetwalker was obsolete. Paying for sex was becoming more like a promotional transaction, with the constant incentive to purchase a host of related services. Who knows what would have happened had I asked Tiffany if I could use her phone?

Just as I was beginning to put these thoughts to rest, the concierge of the hotel waved me over to his desk. He was dressed in a tuxedo, high-collared shirt, and bowtie, although his five o'clock shadow made him look like he had recently been making wanton love.

"Sir, it's the girl you were with. She says she likes you and asks if she can come back up to your room. She is sorry that she had to be on the phone so much, but she promises that if she comes back she won't take any long-distance calls."

I couldn't help myself.

"Oh, of course. Tiffany." He was nonplussed. He plainly wasn't familiar with my pet name for prostitutes. I wanted to explain to him that it was a little like the euro, that having a universal name for all sex workers was a form of globalism that facilitated commerce.

"Is she for real?" I asked.

"Yes, for *reals*," he misinterpreted. "She's a working girl, but

I can tell she really likes you. I know that girl and she wouldn't give up her long-distance calls for just anyone."

I knew there were a million girls who would love to have my *reals*. Brazil is a land where flesh is cheap, but I was afraid that despite all the possibilities available, I could end up empty-handed after my first day in Rio, waking up in the morning to an empty bed. I would be like the Buridan's ass of medieval philosophy, which ended up starving or dying of thirst because it couldn't decide whether it wanted hay or water. "Send her up," I told the concierge.

Before I knew it, Tiffany was back in my room guaranteeing in broken English that she only had three more phone calls to make. Absence makes the heart grow fonder, and with all my waiting I was now ready for a hot night of lovemaking. I called down to the concierge and told him that I would need Tiffany for the whole night, no matter what the cost. I figured that despite the language barrier, I couldn't get bored with all the activities—fellatio, nude dancing, doggy style, missionary—I had picked from the menu. I didn't count on the fact that Tiffany would treat my room like it was her office.

In fact, by the end of the evening Tiffany had so many calls coming in, and was carrying on so much business with swarthy teenaged boys who dropped off packages that looked like everything from stock certificates to hard drugs, that I seriously thought of taking another room just so I could get some sleep. The most interesting part of our evening together was that it was very much like a real relationship. I wanted sex and Tiffany was continually too busy for it. The one time we actually did try to have sexual intercourse in the doggy style that I prefer, she was, from what I could tell, on the phone with a Chinese pharmaceutical company in which she apparently owned a small interest. She shook free of me during a particularly heated exchange with her Chinese counterparts, before I had time to finish. I couldn't help remarking how the circumstances reflected our new global economy. The only word of Chinese that Tiffany knew was something that sounded like "gong," and from what I could tell, her counterparts weren't fluent in Portuguese, so both sides were forced to speak broken English. There had been several news reports about contaminated shipments of the blood thinner Heparin, which was produced in China, and I hoped for Tiffany's sake that the company she had invested in was not one of those involved.

Besides sex, one of my obsessions is clean air, and I try to engage in sexual acts that don't release any toxins into the atmosphere. So I was a little bit upset when, amidst all the telephoning, Tiffany pulled out a cigarette and lit up. Never mind that it was a non-smoking room, Tiffany was violating environmental standards that I frankly supported. This was the only moment during our night of thwarted passion that I felt serious tension, despite our differing ideas about the *quid pro quo* of the hooker/client transaction. It was just a night, but who's to say that what we were experiencing was not a relationship? Like many couples, we were having a conflict over values, and I didn't want to tell her (and couldn't, since I didn't speak Portuguese) that I was glad the extent of our issues was limited to smoking. Larger questions of religious affiliation or belief in God trip up so many couples. In fact, this is the benefit of the so-called one-night stand (especially when the sex is for hire): you get all the intimacy of a relationship without the side effects.

Tiffany's negotiations with the Chinese pharmaceutical company continued late into the night, and even though she was kind enough to conduct most of her affairs while sitting on the toilet with the bathroom door closed, I could hear her scream out "O-la!" in disgust at what I supposed was some piece of bad news. The gorgeous sunrise over the Copa was, of course, not visible from my hotel room window, which, beyond the two ten-ton condensing units, faced another bank of hotel rooms whose occupants were also fated to miss the ocean view. I sometimes think that there should be a support group for people who, like myself, are always missing something.

I awakened to find Tiffany snoring softly next to me. We hadn't negotiated how much of the night would be allotted to torrid sex and how much to sleep. In any case, we didn't have a chance to complete the one sex act we had begun thanks to the distractions of the Chinese pharmaceutical industry. In the morning she slept late, and by the time she got up, I was already coming back from the gym. I returned to find her sitting in front of an enormous breakfast from room service, switching channels between Portuguese versions of the VH1 series "I Love New York" and HBO's "In Treatment."

I could have left Tiffany in the room all day. I'm sure she would have been happy to watch television while fielding calls from China, or wherever else she had invested her money. Tiffany was essentially offering phone sex, in that she was always on the phone and didn't mind occasionally performing sexual acts while she was talking, as long as they didn't interrupt her conversation. I was actually developing an affection for Tiffany, but knew there were other women to meet in Rio. I wanted to play the field, so I told her she had to leave. I didn't want to be rude or hurt her feelings, so I just said, "*Meine Mutter kommt*," and she got the idea.

Tiffany quickly packed up her things and, as she grabbed the money from my hands, I realized that she was probably annoyed with me because she wouldn't be leaving the room with her phone fully charged.

Once she was gone, I breathed a deep sigh of relief and returned to the lobby. My concierge friend was no longer there, so I decided I would just go out onto the Copa and try my luck again. I saw several pretty *senhoras* in the signature swimwear I had come to expect in Rio. From a rational standpoint, the thongs that barely cover Brazilian women's private parts make complete economic sense—if you want to sell goods, you have to display them. I walked out onto the beach, taking in a deep whiff of the early morning smells of garbage, diesel oil, and sewage that were blowing in from the city. Surely this was paradise.

I felt a little overdressed in my Brooks Brothers seersucker suit and bowtie, but I was hoping I might run into some old-fashioned hookers, the kind who didn't go in for Brazilian waxing. I like prostitutes with hairy bushes and quaint values, and I was hoping that my formal attire might attract the kind of passionate, fulsome whores who were fixtures in Cuba during the Batista era, when Havana was a wide open city and the renowned Superman was displaying his outsized genitals in the nightclubs.

I passed a tall buxom woman with bleached blond hair who didn't look like one of the natives at all. "Hi, Tiffany," I said. She swung around in one quick, brutal movement. From the moment I saw her face, I could see that everything about her was fake. She had huge Botoxed lips that looked like they might explode. Even her nose, and in particular her nostrils, which flared like those of a horse, looked like they had been injected with some substance designed to counteract the sagging of age. She was the female version of Dorian Gray.

I don't know what I expected. I'm aware there are some Latin women with fair complexions who have the look of tawdry Vegas showgirls, but I was totally taken aback by her accent, which placed her as a native of one of New York's outer boroughs. If we hadn't been in Rio, and she hadn't camouflaged her age with Botox, I would have sworn that she was the grown-up version of a girl I made out with in Kew Gardens twenty-five years back. "How did you know my name?" she said with a nasal twang. "Are you a cop?"

"I thought you were someone else. You look like Tiffany Spears." As I watched Tiffany walk away, I was going to call out to her. She was walking onto the beach, having forgotten to take off her stiletto heels, and before I could say anything she had gotten stuck in the sand. I noticed her kneeling down to pull her feet out of her shoes and then trying to extricate the shoes themselves, whose heels might as well have been nails.

When I returned to the lobby of the hotel to get my bearings, the concierge waved me over to tell me about a sexy promotional offer. If I changed my return ticket so that I flew back to New York on TAM, the airline of Brazil, I could upgrade the status of my hotel room.

"But I had a roundtrip ticket on Continental."

"I know, Mr. Cantor."

"Call me Ken."

"Okay, Ken. If you change to the TAM flight, you get the room upgrade and you are still saving money. It's a terrific promotion."

This concierge's name was Victor, and we were beginning to have the kind of relationship in which I grow close to someone because they are saving me money.

"Oh my God, there's the French art critic who fucks everybody!" Victor yelped suddenly.

Victor's eyes were like radar, helping me to hone in on a sexy woman in platform shoes and gold lamé skirt walking toward one of the elevator banks. I recognized her as the author of several sexually charged memoirs about her life in art. She would have looked just like a hooker if it weren't for her peasant blouse. I was sure she wasn't wearing a bra; it was the one thing that beatniks and whores from Rio had in common.

"Go run after her, Ken. She's very hot. Sometimes she can't even make it up to her room. If you're lucky, she might even fuck you in the elevator on the way up. The other day we had to kick her out of the men's room when she was reaching into the urinals for men's penises. She's very hot."

I dutifully followed her, but I was hesitant because I tend to be more discriminating about my art criticism than I am about my whores, and I was afraid I might find myself *in flagrante delicto* with someone whose opinions I didn't cotton to. While I covet the female figure, I don't care for champions of figuration.

I managed to jump into the elevator right behind her. She was wearing sunglasses, and for a moment I thought she didn't even notice me, though we had the elevator entirely to ourselves. One of her books was a bestseller about her experiences taking on truckloads of men in the parking lots of museums. Maybe seeing art put her into a heightened state—what some psychoanalysts have termed the Stendhal Syndrome or hyperkulturemia. Apparently she needed to get gangbanged every time she reviewed a show. After five or six floors of her seeming indifference, I began to fear I was the exception, the one man she didn't feel compelled to use for sexual relief. It was only after we zoomed past the fifteenth floor and my eardrums began to pop that she pulled up her skirt and asked, "Do you want to play with my twat?" in a heavy French accent.

"Oh, you speak English!"

"Yes. So you'll understand what I mean when I say I want your balls in my mouth."

I felt embarrassed to say no, but I suddenly realized I had come to Brazil for the prostitution, not to have free sex with a French intellectual. I wanted a Rio whore. When she saw that I was not interested, she hiked her skirt up even higher and started to jerk herself off, which created the requisite degree of excitement in me. For a moment I toyed with the notion of a circle jerk, but I was committed to enjoying the manners and mores of the country I was visiting, and I didn't want to do in the heart of Rio what I could readily accomplish in an elevator in New York. Before I could make any decisions about how to proceed, the elevator reached my floor and I decided to leave her to her own devices.

I'd fucked street whores all over the world, and whether in Paris, London, Prague, or Dublin, I'd only been with whores who were in it for the money. Only Rio had a reputation for having prostitutes who really *enjoyed* making love to their customers, and who were capable of forming true relationships, in which money, albeit important, was not the only part of the picture. They often say women marry men for money, but that doesn't mean that they can't love them. Of course the prostitutes in Rio wanted to be paid, just like anywhere else, but this wasn't proof that at some point along the way they couldn't create a loving relationship, however brief. For every Tiffany there was a john, and, hopefully, a Ken. Now that I was on the verge of being upgraded to more sumptuous digs, I could get down to the real purpose of my visit, which was to find a satisfactory, even ecstatic form of love for hire.

On my way back into the hotel from one of my earlier excursions out to the Copa, I'd noticed busloads of scholarly looking men wearing horn-rimmed glasses, unloading outside the lobby. I later learned that the hotel was hosting an international convention of psychoanalysts, and that many of the events, which were to be held in English, would be open to the public. I have always been interested in psychoanalysis because it deals with two of the things I tend to obsess about: love and work. Maybe attending some of the lectures might be of help as I struggled to find the perfect Tiffany. My interest in psychoanalysis dated from my days as a Scout. I wanted to be an analyst the way some kids want to be rock stars, and I even stood in front of the mirror and had fantasies of being cheered on by the huge crowds that accompanied Freud's first and only trip to the US, when he gave lectures at Clark University. Even after I became an accountant, I toyed with the idea of being a lay analyst, that is, someone who practices without an MD degree. I was young, and it seemed like a great way to get laid.

Now, as I walked through the lobby, I noticed a chef splitting coconuts with a large machete in front of one of the auditoriums, where a poster advertised that morning's lecture, "Ego Splitting, Homeopathy and Psychopathy in Adolescent and mid-life Peyronie's Patients." The abstract beneath read simply, "The effect of a crooked penis on the male psyche will be explored." I decided to give it a try.

Walking into the auditorium, I could see a lot of empty seats. The few people in attendance looked more like curious hotel staff than professionals, and I realized that most of the analysts had probably gone to the beach in search of sun and fun. While the presenter, Dr. Arnold Sunshine, was setting up his PowerPoint presentation, a short woman in what looked like a blond wig sat down next to me. She was wearing polka-dot hot pants, a tight halter-top, and heels so high they were feats of structural engineering. Most of the female analysts I had met back in Manhattan had severe-looking cropped hair and wore smock dresses. This being an international conference, I knew that many cultures would be represented, and I wouldn't have been surprised to find that the distaff members of the Brazilian analytic establishment dressed like whores. I also wouldn't have been the least surprised if they had names like Tiffany. The woman in the polka-dot hot pants leaned over and blew in my ear, murmuring something that I didn't understand. Figuring that it was an important analytic issue having to do with the conference, I motioned her to follow me out to my concierge friend, who would be able to translate.

She repeated to him what she had said to me.

"Uh, the translation is: 'Getting fucked in my hot cunt drives me crazy,'" Victor whispered slyly. I figured she must be a working girl, so I responded politely by saying, "Thank you, Tiffany, but I'm otherwise occupied."

When I got back to the ballroom, the lights had been turned down and Sunshine's PowerPoint presentation had begun. On the screen was a picture of a crooked penis.

I noticed that the audience, though small, seemed intent on Sunshine's lecture. Did they allow themselves to feel any stimulation or to entertain any prurient thoughts of their own, even if as analysts they were supposed to be objective?

After Sunshine had concluded his presentation, there was a little break in which the analysts gathered around a table to have *schnecken* and coffee. It was just like being in New York. Many stragglers must have come in during the slide show, because I noticed that the crowd had thickened and that there was even some degree of competition for the pastries, which seemed to be one of the main attractions for the hungry analysts.

As I bit into a tasty cinnamon *schnecken* with raisins, I found myself staring into the eyes of a petite Asian woman whose breasts spilled out of her tight blouse. She was wearing high-heeled platform shoes and a short skirt.

"Hi, Tiffany," I blurted. "I'm Kenny Cantor from New York." I knew that Brazilians were a mixed race, made up of Portuguese, Spanish, Indian, and sometimes even Asian blood, so it wasn't much of a leap to assume that she might be a Rio whore, even though she looked Chinese or Japanese.

"Perhaps you are mistaking me for someone else. I'm Dr. Dentata. What institute are you with?"

"Well I'm certifiable, if that's any help." Dr. Dentata didn't seem to get the joke. "I'm a CPA."

"Oh, a CPA with analytic training, I find that very interesting. I think that more analysts need to take courses in accountancy. I remember that song that Pete Seeger used to sing: "Well, Doctor Freud, oh Doctor Freud/ How we wish you had been different-ly employed/ But the set of circumstances/ Still enhances the finances/ Of the followers of Doctor Sigmund Freud."

I don't think Dr. Dentata realized how loudly she was singing, because a crowd had gathered around her, several of them humming along to the tune. I half expected one of them to pull out a Fender and start playing the bass line.

After her impromptu concert, Dr. Dentata held out her hand. "Well it was nice talking to you," she said.

"You too, Dr. Dentata."

"Just call me China."

"China Dentata, that sounds like Vagina Dentata, a syndrome in which the vagina is deemed to have teeth, which then turn it into an agent of castration."

"Yes, everyone says that. I don't know what my parents were thinking. My grandparents were among the Japanese who were put in internment camps during the war, but that doesn't explain why my parents didn't name me something more common, like Yoko. They were '60s hippies who took acid and practiced free love, and they were into giving their children unusual names. My father was Dick and they named my brother Moby."

"Well, it was nice to meet you. Goodbye, China." I realized that she was an analyst, and that analysts usually don't have sex with their patients unless they are suffering from very severe counter-transference. But I wasn't her patient—yet.

Despite my childhood fantasies, it may seem odd that a CPA would know so much about psychoanalysis, but I'm from New York, and all educated New Yorkers are experts in psychoanalysis, whether they undergo treatment or not. H. Rap Brown once said violence is as American as cherry pie. Well psychoanalysis is as New York as Pakistani cab drivers. Many German and Viennese analysts who had been refugees from the Nazis settled in Manhattan, which sports as many psychoanalytic institutes as England has soccer teams. The New York Psychoanalytic Institute is the Manchester United of the lot. Growing up in Manhattan in a family with aspirations to be culturally *au courant*, I amassed statistics about psychoanalytic stars like A.A. Brill, Ernest Jones, Sándor Ferenczi, Ernst Kris, and Phyllis Greenacre the way some kids memorized the batting averages of Joe Dimaggio, Yogi Berra, Willie Mays, and Hank Aaron. My favorite was the French analyst Janine Chasseguet-smirgel, author of the tome *Creativity and Perversion*. She was the equivalent of an excellent minor league player, to the extent that her work was only known to the relatively small coterie who collected psychoanalytic memorabilia.

China was carrying one of those quart bottles of Volvic water, which she gulped lasciviously as she entered the central atrium of the hotel. I almost followed her, thinking I might find her turning tricks like so many of the other inhabitants of Rio. I was sure that China was a very good therapist. She was attentive and empathetic, but I was also certain that she could equal if not better her reputation by changing her name to Tiffany and adopting the life of a whore. She had the looks, and every bone in my body told me she had the talent.

Our parting had felt a little like the last scene of *Casablanca*. There was no plane waiting to take her away from me, there was no heroic resistance leader standing between us, no war, and I wasn't a hardened American expatriate named Rick. Yet I felt I could hear the strains of "As Time Goes By" playing on the piano in some beat-up North African café. China—the very name created a frisson.

When would I ever see my China again? It didn't take long to answer the question, as she walked right back into the auditorium, swigging from an even larger bottle of water. I still hadn't decided what my approach was going to be. If I took it for free, we would be in a real relationship, where raw emotion was the currency. And if I became China's patient, I would have to put her in the position of employing the transference in an unethical manner. I felt I needed a therapist just to work out the mess I'd gotten myself into.

Unfortunately, I was again deviating from my plan. I was well into my second day in Rio without having enjoyed the abundance that was supposed to be everywhere, if I was to believe the sex tourism guides and online reviews of Rio nightlife. When I had first considered taking my vacation in Rio, I had simply Googled "Rio + prostitution." The sheer number of results, along with the four-star ratings and exuberant descriptions, had played a large role in my booking a flight.

But all was not lost. Even though I hadn't yet gotten what I came for, the psychoanalytic conference being held at the hotel was a welcome, frequently titillating diversion. I had a lump in my throat as I read the notices for the afternoon panels: "The Oldest Profession: the Neuro-Anatomy of Streetwalking" and "Working Girls: Parallels in Phone Sex and Telephone Analysis."

Now is probably as good a time as any to talk about how a nice Jewish boy like me came to spend most of his adult life with prostitutes. It was really very simple. From an early age, I knew there was something wrong with me. I didn't have any friends, and no girls seemed to like me. But the sluttiest girl in my high school class, Janet Borges, agreed to go to the senior prom with me. With thick lips, smudged from countless make-out sessions, and huge tits, she was crudely sexy. She always wore a short cheerleader skirt with no underpants, even though she wasn't a cheerleader. Most of the members of the school's varsity football team had fucked her, and no one considered her respectable prom material. I purchased the usual corsage, which was the price I had to pay for my first fuck in life.

We started to see each other the summer of my senior year, before I started college, and one night I jokingly offered her money for sex, which she unjokingly took, saying, "I never thought you would ask." Besides the fact that our sex, which had been tentative up until then, took off into a whole new stratosphere, it was the beginning of her career as whore and mine as a john.

By my freshman year in college, Janet was fully set up in the business, and so successful that I realized my heart would be broken unless I started to play the field and see other whores. My first analysis in my twenties had enabled me to break with my mother. My father was a business type, and my mother and I had a confidant relationship in which she talked to me about things that my father wasn't interested in, like emotions and art. The analysis had gotten me to the point of addressing my early inclination to pay for sex. Had I continued, I might have been able to form a relationship with a woman that wasn't a monetary transaction. I had made the transition from the mother/confidant to the mother/whore figure, which was a great leap, but I was aware there were other feelings toward women that had yet to be added to the palette.

I was an ambitious young man, and shortly after I graduated from college I had already drummed up enough business to support a Midtown accountancy office manned by a staff of loyal employees. Who had the time or the money to see an analyst four days a week? But in the end, this is precisely what I would do, as I returned to analysis repeatedly over the years. However, the Rio conference was enabling me to view analysis from a different perspective. I had always been limited to the patient's point of view, which is mostly prone. But here I was seeing analysts eye-to-eye, watching them as they exchanged valuable insights with each other. I was seeing the kind of people they really were.

If I had met China in a professional situation, in which she demonstrated analytic neutrality, she would simply have been a very good-looking Asian piece of ass. At worst, I might have tried to look up her skirt during my initial intake. I would have stared at her platform heels and wondered to myself *what kind of an analyst wears shoes like that?* I probably would have thought something like *I bet she's a really good fuck.* I might even have communicated these thoughts to her in the course of a session, and we would have dealt with it as part of the transference.

My last analyst, Sam Johnson, was a short man who had such thick stubble that he always looked unshaven, though he was very proper. He wore industrial grade, rubber-soled shoes, blue blazers and gray pants, and rarely said anything. I frequently communicated to him my perception that he was a virgin whom no woman would ever go near. I discovered on the Internet that he was married and had children, but I still had fantasies about his private life. My previous analytic work had gotten me used to indulging in fantasy and free-association, even when I wasn't in treatment. For instance, I was sure that even if Victor the concierge seemed like a normal male, he was a secret cross-dresser who hid his penis between his legs when he was putting on women's panties.

But getting back to China, I had gone so far as to imagine the moment in our first consultation when she would suggest I move to the couch. Was I to take this as an invitation to classic Freudian analysis, or to sex? Maybe her chaise longue was little more than a proverbial casting couch.

My reverie about China was interrupted when I saw Dr. Sunshine return to the auditorium. He was surrounded by a coterie of followers, bearded men in wool suits who looked like they had stepped out of turn-of-the-century Vienna and could easily have been members of Freud's inner circle. I even overheard some conversations in what sounded like German, though many New York analysts talk so quickly and enigmatically that it is often difficult to tell what language they're speaking. I wanted to introduce myself to Sunshine, but as he walked by I had a Tourettic moment, emitting a muffled, involuntary cry of "Daddy!"

It turned out that Sunshine was a charismatic and controversial figure whose attempts to broaden the audience for Freud's insights had included showing '70s porn films, with famous stars like John Holmes, Harry Reems, and Linda Lovelace, as illustrations of his theories of narcissism and idealization. Sunshine had been brought up in an orthodox Jewish family in the Borough Park section of Brooklyn. His parents had actually been members of the Satmar sect, led by Moses Teitelbaum and his feuding sons, Aaron and Zalman. Sunshine was not a practicing Jew, but he was no stranger to feuds. The once close relationship with his student David Moldauer had fractured over the fundamental aim and purpose of using pornographic films to illustrate his theories, mirroring the famous split between Freud and his Aryan disciple, Jung. (Sunshine's famous maxim, "We aim to please, will you aim too, please?" displayed above the toilet in his office bathroom, was another bone of contention between the two men).

The position once occupied by Moldauer had been taken over by someone named Herbert Schmucker. Schmucker had a whole theory of Oedipal rivalry that argued it was best to be as blatant about it as possible. This explained the fact that he named his institute after himself instead of after his esteemed mentor, Sunshine, and favored a porn film entitled *Three Some*, in which a physically appealing couple invite their sad-sack friend to watch them having sex, while never allowing him to join in. Schmucker had argued on more than one occasion that sexual satisfaction derives from a feeling of superiority in getting something that someone else doesn't have. The guilt from such feelings of rivalry, he believed, is what any good analysis should attempt to alleviate. There were all kinds of paradoxes in analysis. For instance, one of the most famous centers for the study of analysis in Manhattan is the Karen Horney Clinic, but what kind of inducement is a name like that? How could Karen Horney help me? Why wouldn't I go to a place honoring someone named Karen Un-Horney, where the name at least held out a hope?

Sunshine and Schmucker were like an argumentative married couple. Over the remainder of my stay in Rio, I would frequently find them sniping at each other in the halls, and in one case overheard a furious battle in which Sunshine actually brought up the naming of Schmucker's institute, telling Schmucker in a petulant voice that could be heard throughout the hotel lobby, "You're behaving like you just got off the boat. You're behaving just like a schmuck!" Indeed, I learned from Wikipedia that Schmucker's parents had been humble German immigrants, and that Schmucker had grown up in the Yorkville section of Manhattan. Schmucker's parents had occupied a tenement on 86th Street above the Old Heidelberg restaurant. But the old German neighborhood was in the same district as the silk-stocking PS 6 (which I would attend years later) and Schmucker was able to get an education that allowed him to rise out of his immigrant roots, attend medical school at NYU, and eventually become a prominent psychoanalyst.

China had been close-lipped when Sunshine had come up in our conversation, but she spoke with great reverence about Schmucker, whom she plainly regarded as one of the gods of Olympus. It was clear from her attitude that Sunshine had become a mere footnote in the arc of Schmucker's career.

I returned to the lobby to look for Victor the concierge. He hadn't been much help, but it has always been my philosophy that it's good to do the same thing again and again even if it fails to produce results. I remember my analyst telling me that there are people who in fact unconsciously want to bring about the outcomes they so often complain about. There is even a word for it in the psychoanalytic literature: parapraxis.

I was thrown into a tailspin when I arrived at the concierge desk to find that Victor wasn't there. In his place was a small, dark, unshaven man with the face of a rodent. I immediately dubbed him Rat Man, after Freud's famous patient. His nametag read, "Adolphe." When I asked when Victor was coming back, Adolphe was evasive. He pulled the language card, pretending he didn't understand what I was saying. As far as Adolphe was concerned, he was the concierge now and Victor didn't exist anymore. I felt very much the way I did years before when my analyst got sick and set me up with a dentist named Dr. Klein, a good friend of his who had had analytic training, but for some reason had chosen to become a dentist instead. For months I went to Klein's office on 57th Street, using his dental chair as an analytic couch. As then, I dreaded having to tell my story all over again, especially to someone like Adolphe, who didn't seem to be the kind of person with whom I could be comfortable expressing my desires. In the middle of this awkwardness, Schmucker appeared. He seemed already to know Adolphe well.

"Ah yes, Dr. Schmucker, the patient is waiting in your room." There was something oddly unsubtle about Adolphe. The way he addressed Schmucker made it apparent that the word "patient" was a euphemism for what in all likelihood was a Tiffany.

I have always been a kind of groupie when it comes to mental health professionals, so I impulsively put out my hand as Schmucker turned in my direction. When I said, "I'm Kenny Cantor from New York and I've really been enjoying your conference—especially the films," he gave me a withering look that communicated exactly how irrelevant I was to him. I could see he was perspiring profusely, so I figured he was already somewhat worked up about the "patient" who was waiting for him in his room.

"So, Adolphe, give me the real run-down on what happened to Victor," I said, after Schmucker had hustled off to his assignation. "Did they can him?"

"All major canning companies in Brazil are in the São Paulo area."

"No, *can* is an American expression that means *fire*. You 'fire' someone when you remove him from his job and tell him he can't work for you anymore. You can also say a *senhora* has a nice 'can.'"

Adolphe responded with an expression that was equal parts confusion and bemusement. I pointed to a cream-colored Tiffany who looked like she was just coming on for her evening shift and seemed to have a condition, more common in Africa than Brazil, called steatopygia, which is a distended rear end. It was a deformity, but it illustrated my point.

"For instance that *senhora* with the tight pants has quite a can," I said.

"One hundred dollars American," Adolphe shot back.

"I admire her extension, which reminds me of a guest house attached to a larger estate. But I'm looking for your normal sexy Brazilian whore with a nice butt. I'm all for helping people with their troubles, but one thing I learned in my years of therapy is that you don't have sex with someone because you feel sorry for them. Anyway, it's a big world out there and there is always going to be some john who likes the chick with overly large this or that or none at all. I once heard of a prostitute who had a vagina with no hole, and she had plenty of customers, believe it or not. She'd had some kind of industrial accident before she became a working girl, and all her orifices had to be put in different places. I think she peed from her belly button and went to a gynecologist when she had a toothache. I know it sounds totally unbelievable, but apparently there was a harmonious logic to her whole body. So, Adolphe, tell me, where are all the good Tiffanys?"

I leaned over conspiratorially. Adolphe looked in both directions to see if anyone was listening and whispered, "Victor is now the bartender at The Café Gringo. It's very dark in there, but he will get you nice girls."

I was so happy that Victor had found gainful employment that I stopped feeling horny and frustrated for a moment, although when I thought of Herbert Schmucker making passionate love to a Tiffany in his room, I was filled with penis envy.

I was sure I saw the face of an Asian woman in a crowd of people waiting for the elevators at the end of the lobby, and my heart skipped a beat thinking it might be China. It was at that point that I understood something that neuroscientists have known for years: our emotions are often ahead of our thoughts. I was more involved with China than I could have possibly realized, and was already feeling troubled by the prospective complexities we would face. I have looked into the eyes of dogs and cats, and I know there is a tendency to anthropomorphize them, to believe that somehow they are thinking about you. China almost had the opposite effect on me. When I'd looked into her eyes I saw a hungry animal with only a veneer of culture, consciousness, and sensibility. I had the urge to dart across the lobby, if only to stand next to her in the elevator, if only to feel the warmth of her body close to mine. I seethed with jealousy when I imagined that the patient waiting for Schmucker in his room was not a Tiffany at all, but China Dentata. As it happened, the Asian woman I had spotted across the lobby was indeed China—en route, I assumed in my jealous delirium, to Schmucker's room. Analysis was just like every other profession—good-looking women routinely fucked their way to the top.

But I stopped myself before I could go any further. If China and Schmucker were an item, standing next to her in the elevator and wishing her a nice afternoon would get me nowhere, unless I had some chloroform and a pair of handcuffs. Having neither, I elected to continue with my original plan and head off to The Gringo to consult with Victor. There was no sense in chasing windmills. I realized I was coming deathly close to having my seven days in Rio turn into nothing more than my other 358 days in New York, where all my interactions with Tiffanys were fraught with anxiety.

My heart was in my throat as the doors opening onto the Copa swished open. It was late afternoon. I imagined China in the arms of Schmucker, their writhing bodies in an almost perfect psychoanalytic embrace, in which love and work, like the stars in a John Donne poem, were "perfectly conjoined." I started mentally undressing the women who now paraded themselves before me. I had been thinking I ought to get one of those sandwich boards they use to shill discount suits in Manhattan. Mine would say, "American with *Reality* Seeks Available Girls." Not everyone would get it, but enough so that I would enhance my selection. As it was, I noticed so many Tiffanys in tiny thongs that I didn't know which one to pick first.

I assumed that as an attractive, partially psychoanalyzed American with *reals*, every Tiffany would be after me. But it was no use even trying. It was a situation that is known in psychoanalytic literature as a double bind, in which the patient gets conflicting messages. If I wanted to get attention I had to advertise it, but if I advertised it I would get more propositions than I could handle. Besides, I had begun to develop an indifference toward the Rio girls, which, even if it was manufactured in my head, was becoming stronger by the minute. The fact that I couldn't get my first Tiffany off the phone with her Chinese clients probably didn't help matters. I have learned that experiences of this kind can traumatize a patient, or a john, and shape his view of the world.

I turned to a Tiffany standing to my right and asked, "*Senhora*, do you know a place called The Gringo?" She was gorgeous, and even though I knew her body was for sale, I figured she was like one of those Michelin five-star restaurants where you have to make a reservation years in advance. She had olive-colored skin, dark braided hair, and a perfect chin. She was a "10." In fact she looked like a Latin version of the character Bo Derek played in the movie. Her breasts stood perfectly motionless, like soldiers at attention. I decided to take a businesslike attitude, holding out my hand and introducing myself.

"By the way, Tiffany, I'm Ken Cantor." It turned out she spoke very good English, but I can't remember what she said, since I was too flabbergasted by the fact that someone so spectacularly beautiful was talking to me. This Tiffany was no mere whore. She was a call girl, an escort, a courtesan. Whatever the highest rank one can give to someone who sells her body, she deserved it.

Tiffany looked me up and down like she was inspecting a new car. Deep inside I maintained the hope that she would say, "You don't need to go to The Gringo. Why don't you come back to my apartment?" Though there are lots of Tiffanys in

Rio, the kind of Tiffany I was looking at was a rarity, and could surely command top dollar, or *real*, as was the case. For her it was always a seller's market. I was sure that she occupied a lavish condo with a balcony overlooking the Copacabana. She was not a whore who worked out of one of those dingy hotel rooms with hourly rates.

"Oh yes, I am quite familiar with The Gringo," she said with a smile. It was only when I noticed her voice was a little lower than I expected, and saw that she had an Adam's apple, that I realized she was a man, one of the legion of beautiful pre-op transsexuals who are a famous feature of Rio nightlife.

Even though Tiffany was more beautiful than any woman I had ever encountered, I didn't need something stiff and hard when that's what I already had. It's like meeting someone who thinks just the way you do. At first you get excited about finding a like mind, then boredom sets in as you anticipate every word they say. It's what's known as prolepsis in the world of rhetoric, and I hadn't flown five thousand miles to experience an evening of it in phallic form.

It turned out The Gringo was located across the road that ran along the Copacabana, in a warren of side streets that were plastered with flashing neon signs shaped in the forms of palm trees and half-naked females. The streets were lined with old hotels whose doorways were filled with bored-looking Tiffanys. For a moment, like Orpheus, I had the desire to turn back for my Eurydice. Looking around, I was suddenly filled with premonitions of disaster, and this last Tiffany's Adam's apple had a reassuring appeal. She was just one of the guys, after all. I imagined what it would be like to massage her breasts. At the same time, I had disturbing thoughts about her penis. People solicited pre-ops because they presented a buffet of sexual pleasures. If you had homosexual inclinations or were AC/DC, you got the pleasure of being able to indulge all of your desires at the same time. Taking a democratic point of view, I asked myself, "Why not?" Before long I was imagining what it would be like to put Tiffany's big cock in my mouth or to have her hardened nipples gently tickle my back as I felt something hard nudging my ass.

I quickly silenced my deviant thoughts and proceeded into what was apparently one of Rio's most vice-infested areas, an area where, I was told, everything was permitted, making the old Havana of the '50s, with its cock-wielding Superman and naked sex clubs, look like Mr. Roger's neighborhood. In short, I was headed into an area into which only the most intrepid sex traveler dared to venture.

I'd been so busy dealing with the analytic convention and dismantling the business office that the first Tiffany had set up in my hotel room (in fact I was still fielding calls from China and a number of so-called "emerging markets" where she'd been involved in venture capital deals, including a sub-prime mortgage situation in Uzbekistan), I hadn't had time to lie back and sip on a *caipirinha*. Everywhere I went I saw waiters carrying around exotic drinks with colorful little umbrellas. I knew that if I got a little tipsy I could relax, and in all likelihood find myself surrounded by beautiful Tiffanys before I knew it. I decided that before I got to The Gringo I would stop in the first reasonable-looking bar and have a few drinks to loosen up.

The first place I found was an American bar called The New York Yankees Club House, which broadcast Yankees games on cable. It was midwinter in America and not the time for a Yankees game, but the place looked just like one of those classic Irish taverns, with old men sitting cross-legged on benches, staring up at a television and not saying a word to each other.

"What'll ya have, Mack," the bartender said as I sat down. This place was the real McCoy. They sold "crisps," cheap bags of Planters Peanuts, and hard-boiled eggs, and they had Harp and Guinness on tap. The whole place smelled of urine. I noticed that even though all the regulars looked like Irish doormen out of central casting, the bartender himself, despite his thick Bronx accent, appeared to be a Rio native—dark, slim, and handsome—and not the kind of sallow-faced, beer-bellied creature I was likely to find at a similar establishment in Manhattan.

When I got closer to the television, I noticed that everyone in the bar was watching Bob Hope perform for troops on some aircraft carrier. I quickly surmised that they were watching a tape of one of Hope's overseas performances during the Vietnam War. Bob Hope alternated on the television with some equally musty broadcasts of Yankees games, featuring the sportscaster Phil Rizzuto. I knew this was one place where I wasn't likely to run into any head-turning Tiffanys, but I experienced a moment of homesickness. Back in New York, when I wasn't seeing prostitutes, I enjoyed getting inebriated all by myself, and this was just the kind of place, with cold, inexpensive beer, that I liked to frequent. In fact, I knew that if I wasn't careful, I might end up spending the rest of my time in Rio in this nostalgic dump.

One of the predictable things about Irish bars for someone like me is that the bartender and the patrons always glare suspiciously at newcomers, and I knew that whenever I got up from my stool to take a piss, someone would say perceptive things about me like, "Who the bloody feck is that?" There were a couple of portly fellows with reddened cheeks who looked like retired New York City cops. I figured most of the Irish-doorman types must have been employed in a section of Rio where there were the same kind of elegant pre-war high-rises you find along Park Avenue. This was just the sort of place that you could find in what was left of old Yorkville, with its tenements and mom-and-pop grocery stores.

As I would later learn, most of the Irish doormen at The Club House had been brought down by a Jewish developer who had built several high-rises to cater to the needs of the growing American expatriate community in Rio. He'd felt that the extra New York touch would make his buildings competitive with the towers that had been constructed by Brazilian developers going after the same market.

I'm the kind of guy who can't stop thinking about the one woman who won't talk to him at a party. Instead of moving on when I feel I'm not wanted, I go back for more. So instead of having a beer or two and proceeding on to The Gringo, I set out to win acceptance at The Club House. I was on my third boilermaker when I noticed the other men at the bar swigging down rye with beer chasers. Figuring it would boost my status in the bar, I bought everybody a round. As I started to get inebriated, I began waxing about midnight mass at St Patrick's, even though I'm Jewish. I couldn't stop myself from dropping the name of every Irish-sounding person I knew—O'Kelly, O'Reilly, O'Rourke—while using words like "communion" and "christening" whenever I bought someone a round. My favorite line was, "I'll never forget the time Kennedy went to mass three sheets to the wind. He took the wine with the wafer, but he was wobbling like a ship in a storm…"

In place of Tiffanys, there were just a few pasty-faced sluts with the albinism that comes from the kind of inbreeding that went on in the tight-knit building-services community in Rio. No one can afford a decent Tiffany on a doorman's salary.

I was surprised when I stumbled out into the warm Rio night and heard people speaking Portuguese. During my time in The Club House, I was transported back to New York, and with all the blarney and Killarney and blessed virgin this and that, I imagined I would find myself facing a typical Manhattan street scene, with Bangladeshi cabbies honking at each other. In my inebriated state, I thought I might even run into the ghost of the dearly departed Cardinal O'Connor, whose unforgiving face still decorated some of the Irish pubs along Second Avenue.

I had to pull myself together. Finding Tiffanys was now a job, a mission like the Green Berets ferreting out the Taliban in the mountains of Pakistan. But I was hopelessly adrift in a sea of thought. Lost in my reverie, I had wandered far from my hotel into a strange neighborhood with dangerous-looking, toothless Tiffanys. I had heard about the toothless Tiffanys, who were world-famous for their prodigious talents in the art of oral sex. According to my sex guides, there were all kinds of Tiffanys lurking in Rio's barrios, catering to every imaginable desire, but perhaps it was the danger factor that was causing my procrastination. Many hapless sex tourists had had their wallets snatched from their back pockets on Rio's infamous "Street of Spankings." I had to find my way back to the main drag of sex clubs and bars, where the high-class Tiffanys performed the usual gamut of perversions.

My head was spinning from all the alcohol and I had lost my sense of direction. I thought of the French poet Rimbaud, who welcomed disorientation and looked at the "derangement of the senses" as a higher state of mind, a form of transcendence that he urged upon his readers. But I wasn't looking for poetic inspiration. I didn't need to expand my consciousness. I had to get back down to earth and get laid.

Maybe if I went back into The Club House, the old salt-of-the-earth types, the Finneys, Flahertys, Kennedys, Kilkennys, and Muldoons, might help me to find my way. Even though their revered Catholic church preached abstention and opposed birth control and pre-marital sex, they surely could understand that I was a man with urges that sometimes resulted in sin. I'm sure my friends at the bar would give me an understanding look and simply tell me to go confess my sins to Father Flynn. I could say a hundred Hail Marys and that would be the end of it. I hadn't told any of the guys at the bar I was Jewish, and that was obviously the next step in our relationship. I could just see the faces of the Irish doormen of Rio when I confessed that I represented the Judeo in our Judeo-Christian alliance. From what I could glean, they had ambivalent feelings about Arthur Rosenbaum, the Jewish developer who had imported them from

New York. Many blamed him for separating them from their friends and families back in Yorkville, so I had no guarantee they would take a kindly attitude toward me when they found out who I really was. Racial profiling might be frowned upon in the States, but it was par for the course in Rio. And in a place like The Club House, the patrons proudly lived by their own rules, honor-bound by an unspoken code of conduct that stretched back to the bogs of Ireland.

Scuba diving had been a passion of mine in the days before I devoted myself to the pastime of pursuing beautiful Tiffanys, and I was even PADI certified. Once, diving with an instructor off the beautiful Bahamian island of Eleuthera, I wasn't able to adjust to the depth to which we had plunged, and became completely disorientated. My vision started playing tricks on me, and I saw all manner of fantastical hallucinatory sea creatures. This was precisely the sensation I was now experiencing in this strange part of Rio, where I suddenly came upon species of Tiffany I had never seen before. It's axiomatic that in Rio there are Tiffanys on every corner, but now I was finding wall-eyed Tiffanys, Tiffanys whose bodies were festooned with prosthetic devices, Tiffanys in wheelchairs, blind Tiffanys, Tiffanys who used sign language to bargain. Only this time I couldn't blame it on nitrogen narcosis.

It all reminded me of a very wealthy friend I once knew who couldn't tell the difference between his prostitutes and his wives. His wives had married him for his money, and naturally he lavished money on his prostitutes, but generally the whores ended up costing him less than the wives, and were a lot easier to maintain. Eventually, like me, he began to experience some disorientation, mistaking his wives for hookers and his hookers for wives. It's unclear whether this had any bearing on his tragic demise. He was a licensed flier and died in a freak accident when he lost his bearings during a routine non-instrument landing with a Piper. Apparently, like a dizzy diver, he couldn't tell down from up.

"*Puta, Puta*," came the cry of a woman with a high trembling voice. "Girls, Girls, Girls, Triple X," she said in perfect English. I noticed an old lady in a chair who bore a striking resemblance to Susan Sontag, whose obituary I'd read shortly before leaving for Rio. She had Sontag's striking good looks and the same streak of white in her otherwise jet black hair. I could see that she had once been an attractive Tiffany, just the kind of sex-loving Rio girl I was after. I was thinking about how I could ask her where I could find a girl who looked like her, only younger, without insulting her sexuality. I had heard that Brazilian women remain sexually active until very late in life, and one of the sex-tourism sites even advertised that you could have sex with retired Tiffanys for free. *The Guinness Book of World Records* documents the oldest woman to have had sex as a Brazilian who remained sexually active until she died at 124. She was still having orgasms at 110. Prostitution is the world's oldest profession, but Rio was home to the world's oldest prostitutes.

An intimation of the moon was beginning to appear in the darkening sky, and a solitary street lamp created a scene of desolation that reminded me of an Edward Hopper painting. My mother always told me I was artistic, but she had forced me to choose a secure profession characterized by deadening and repetitive work (her favorite line was, "It's rewarding to work for remuneration"). Apparently, she wanted me to have the kind of steady income that allowed me to take trips to Rio to run after prostitutes. If I had been a struggling artist, I would never have known as many Tiffanys as I had, and I probably would not have found myself staring up at a sign that read "31 Março Revolução." With a start, I realized I was on a street that commemorated one of Rio's most notorious uprisings. Perhaps out of fear, or a need to make a firmer connection with someone who could help me out of the morass I found myself in, I blurted out to the old whore, "Are you by any chance related to Susan Sontag."

"You mean the one who wrote *Against Interpretation*?"

"Yes! And *Styles of Radical Will*, *Illness as Metaphor*, and *Regarding the Pain of Others*, not to mention the novel, *The Death Kit*, and also the movie, *Duet for Cannibals*. Did you know that she directed *Waiting for Godot* in Sarajevo during the bombings?" I knew I was just trying to show off my knowledge, which had never gotten me anywhere and often inspired resentment.

Just as she said, "I lived in the States for many years, but I never became a Sontag fan. I'm a simple woman. I like the kind of art that's about life. I don't buy her whole idea about the autonomy of art," it hit me that I needed more *reality*. I asked her if there was a cash machine nearby. She told me there was one around the corner, but that I should be careful of the *banditos*, who kidnapped American tourists and held them for ransom. I had read a gruesome story about an American who had gotten drunk in a Rio brothel and had been kidnapped by a gang. Though he had finally been released, his penis had been cut off because his wife had refused to pay the ransom.

Though it had probably been a long time since she'd earned the name, I knew this old Tiffany was someone I could talk to. One of the tourist guides indicated that the older Tiffanys often gave good hand jobs when they experienced the kind of vaginal dryness that made repeated sexual intercourse too painful. I could ask her for a hand and even pay her for the trouble.

"I'm a traveler who's become waylaid," I said holding out a *real*. "I'm a little like Odysseus. I started out my journey looking for beautiful prostitutes, but I have been experiencing famine amongst plenty. Now I feel like Robinson Crusoe. Except I haven't been washed up on an island, and consequently have found no Man Friday to show me the way."

"Remember Dorothy in *The Wizard of Oz*?" she asked with a shy smile. "She was told to click her heels together three times and say, 'There's no place like home.' All you have to do is go up to the first good-looking woman you see, click your heels three times, and say, 'Show me your vagina.' Before you know it you will be lying in a hotel bed with a beautiful, young whore. That's all there is to it." She held her hand out and I produced my last wad of *reals*, realizing that I would soon have to take my chances and hit the cash machine she'd directed me to.

I looked down by Tiffany's chair and noticed she was reading Herbert Marcuse's *One-Dimensional Man*. The Marxist tome, which had been popular in the '60s, proposed the theory of "repressive desublimation." It was a book that I was sure was out of print. It would have been hard to come by in Rio or anywhere else. In any case, I imagined it must have once been banned in a country where hedonism was a religion. It was doubly odd to find it in the hands of an aging hooker.

Just then, I noticed two beautiful Tiffanys walking right toward us. "*Senhoras!*" I said, trying as best I could to tamp my eagerness. "Let's get real. Show me your vaginas."

The darker of the two, who seemed an exotic mix of African, Indian, and Asian, walked right up to me.

"You want to see my vagina?" she said in perfect English. "Are you familiar with Gracie Jiu-Jitsu?" It turned out I was looking at two members of Brazil's championship martial arts club, and before I knew it I was indeed staring right at her vagina, from the ground, as she administered a punishing submission.

I had studied enough Jiu-Jitsu when I was in high school to realize that the hold she had me in was like a noose. The more I resisted, the tighter it would become. I wrapped my legs around her waist as I had been taught to do. The next step, as I recalled from my early lessons, was to try to roll her over. But I was starting to enjoy having her on top. It gave me an excellent view down her blouse, the areolae of her lovely breasts just visible over the top of her lacey black brassiere.

I have always liked a little bit of pain. Fingernails clutching at my back, the feeling of being smothered by tight buttocks descending over my face, teeth tugging at my ear, all figure in my repertoire of pleasures. Finding myself on the ground, knowing that my fate was in the hands of a beautiful Tiffany, added to the list of titillations and thrills that constituted my ideal of love. Maybe during the rest of my trip I'd seek out beautiful Tiffanys who would lock me in my hotel room closet, handcuff me to the bed, or just hogtie me for sport. I'd seen the usual S&M imagery—whips, rubber bodices, leather masks, pierced penises and testicles—but I had never so clearly related such esoteric pleasures to my own life. For the most part, my sex life was limited to the missionary position and what is known as "half and half" or "around the world," meaning your basic suck and fuck.

I had previously enjoyed being smothered because it reminded me of my relationship to Mommy, but that really was as far as I would go when it came to sexual experimentation. Now, lying under the light of a street lamp on a deserted Rio street, I felt I was on the verge of experiencing a totally new realm of the senses.

In fact, it reminded me of being bullied as a kid. I would be playing punch ball in the schoolyard, and when it started to get dark a gang of kids would inevitably show up and start pushing us weaker kids around. Robbery was not the real motive, since most of us had empty pockets. These kids came from the local parochial school, where the nuns hit them regularly. They got their pleasure from domination. The panic I felt was that I was never going to escape. Rationally I knew that everyone had to go home for dinner at some point, but when a kid kept pushing me back into the fence every time I tried to leave, or pushed me to the ground and pinned me down, I was overwhelmed with irrational fears.

Adding to my buffet of sensations and memories was the simple fact that I liked the smell of this Tiffany. But if in the end she was just going to practice her Jiu-Jitsu moves on me and never let me pay for sex, I was wasting my time. The trip had already been a learning experience, but I didn't want to be one of those perpetual students, constantly auditing courses but never applying my learning to real-life situations. Right now I was majoring in the ins and outs of the Rio sex industry without having enjoyed any actual sex.

Still, I wasn't about to break out of any of the submissions Tiffany had me in, which she seemed to enjoy alternating every two or three minutes. I figured at least I was doing a good turn by helping her to show off her moves to her friend. Ultimately, I have faith in the goodness of humankind, and I was sure she would let me go when she was through with me.

I must have blacked out in one of her chokeholds. When I came to I found myself lying alone in the middle of the street. I had the feeling I sometimes get when I wake up with a strange dream, still at the edge of consciousness. Luckily, my Susan-Sontag-and-Herbert-Marcuse-reading friend appeared, having seen everything. When I asked her what had happened, she remarked, "They always wrestle johns on the way to practice." Slowly, the finale of my wrestling bout started to come back to me like a grainy black and white film. Tiffany had maneuvered me into yet another chokehold, and I was really having trouble breathing. At the same time, she had me in such a position that her breasts were right in my face, and I was so turned on that I didn't care if I lived or died. I noticed that my pants were wet and realized that I'd either peed on myself out of fear or shot my wad, though the burning sensation on my leg made me think it must have been the former. In any case, I had probably passed out from sheer ecstatic relief.

Before I left New York, I'd read a horrible story about a teenager who accidentally hung himself while trying to masturbate in a state of semi-asphyxiation. The thrill of danger and the lack of oxygen were meant to create a superlative, self-induced high. Here I was, inadvertently finding myself in a life-threatening situation brought about by sexual urges I couldn't control. I didn't want to die, but the delicious confinement and unimaginably pleasurable pain I had experienced had obviously left an imprint on the neurogenic pathways of my brain. If I started to seek out dangerous situations with other Amazonian Tiffanys, I would have to make an appointment for a consultation with an expert like Herbert Schmucker or, better yet, China Dentata, although I might feel timid telling China about my ecstatic ejaculations.

"I just want to get to The Gringo to have a good time," I said, wiping the dirt off my seersucker suit. I straightened my bowtie. The problem I had now—the cross I had to bear—was the conspicuous stain in my crotch. Even the most freewheeling Tiffany, as accustomed to touching, smelling, and swallowing semen as the average woman is to bubble baths, would look askance at a john sporting an egregious cum- or urine-stained crotch. The kind of john who is so horny that he has accidents before he even starts to have sex usually turns out to be a compulsive who may be interested in violent sexual practices. I realized that before I set foot in The Gringo I probably would need to change my pants. I had a hunch that The Gringo could turn into a hub for me, the way Newark is for Continental or Minneapolis-St. Paul for Northwest. If I was going to catch my connecting fucks at The Gringo, I had to start out on the right foot. I wanted to walk in strong and self-assured, not apologizing for an unseemly crotch. For johns and Tiffanys alike, appearances are everything. I may know all about Susan Sontag, Gilles Deleuze, and the *anti-Oedipus*, but the average Tiffany won't care about my erudition when she spots me standing at the bar sporting a crotch stain. In fact, my education had never really produced results when it came to my relationships with Tiffanys. In all my years frequenting dens of sensuality, I had never found that my intellectual credentials got me better-looking girls or discounted fees.

You never know what is going to come out in conversation. That is one of the basic principles I learned in my years of psychoanalysis. When I first went into treatment, I had no inkling of all the shit that existed inside of me, both literally and metaphysically. One of the first reactions I had to analysis was that I couldn't stop going to the bathroom. It went on for days. No sooner had my intestines quieted down than all the excreta of my childhood, which had been forgotten in the bowels of my personality, pressed insistently for immediate evacuation.

I noticed the old, used-up literary Tiffany staring at me quizzically. "How are you enjoying the Marcuse?" I blurted out, apropos of nothing.

"I love all these Marxist guys from the Frankfurt school, but I was finding it hard to concentrate with all the hullabaloo," she shot back, a wry grin curling her lips.

"You don't happen to know of a decent dry cleaner who does spot work?"

"With your American dollars you're almost better off buying a new pair of pants."

It turned out that in addition to her life as a hooker and displaced New York intellectual, Tiffany ran a haberdashery out of her brothel. She had a few samples of her wares right there in her doorway. It turned out she had been married to a garmento named Sammy Cohen, who had manufactured piece goods in a loft on 37th Street and who was, in fact, a major supplier of trouser legs. She knew all about the kind of Brooks Brothers seersucker suit I was wearing.

"I don't know if I can match them exactly, but I can give you something that will get you through the night, and then I'll set you up with a real Hong Kong-style tailor tomorrow."

Tiffany laid aside her book and led me up a rickety flight of stairs. Even though she was an old woman, she was still practiced in having a man follow her into the grimy room she used to turn tricks. She had varicose veins and walked with a slight limp, but still had the air of a lady of the night ready to weave a magic spell over her john. There are certain men who are attracted to older women, and I was sure that Tiffany had her loyal clientele, even if I knew I wasn't going to be one of them. I was prepared to walk out if she started taking her clothes off. As it happened, I was the one doing the undressing in the stark room, with its single cot and scattered piles of washcloths. The only touch of color was provided by one of those old posters of Che Guevara in his signature beret, making the place look like my Columbia dorm room circa 1967.

Tiffany told me to take my pants off while she dragged a big box of garments out of a closet and started to root through it for slacks. I was afraid she was going to offer to throw in a little favor at no extra charge, maybe a blowjob to go with my new slacks.

I had removed my pants and was standing in my boxers. I still had on my seersucker jacket, my button-down collar shirt, and my bowtie when she instructed me to take everything off.

"We have to work from the bottom up in a case like this."

I tend to be shy, hiding myself under the sheets even in the presence of the most immodest Tiffany, so I just imagined I was going to my internist for an annual check-up. I soon found myself standing buck-naked in front of her with my hands crossed chastely over my crotch. I suddenly had more sympathy for women in similar situations who had more goods to hide. She threw me a tiny pair of black bikini briefs. I had never even worn a jockstrap, and when I put on the briefs, with a modest piece of cloth in front and narrower strip at the rear, I felt like the victim of a wedgie. Next came the pants, a pair of bell-bottom jeans with fake rhinestones running down the leg that looked like they had been part of the wardrobe for *Saturday Night Fever*. I'd had the impression Tiffany would be providing me with a duplicate pair of conservative-looking slacks, but the jeans she produced were so tight that they cut off the circulation to my groin. I was afraid that they would cause my penis to become gangrenous, but Tiffany assured me that this was a popular style of dress in Rio.

"If you wear these, the nice Tiffanys will know you are looking for them. But before you go to The Gringo, you should go to The Catwalk. It's an old-fashioned club that used to be in Havana when Batista was alive. All the girls are totally naked, and they even have a Superman who fucks the young virgins live onstage. There you will find many girls who will show you their vaginas. In fact, that is all they do. If nothing else, you have to see it because it's one of the most famous sites in Rio. It's like the Eiffel Tower of sex."

"But I'm not just interested in seeing vaginas," I cried out. "I want to make love." I was surprised at the vehemence of my protestations. From a psychoanalytic point of view, my strong reaction was a sign of conflict. As Queen Gertrude says in *Hamlet*, "The lady doth protest too much, methinks."

Even though the new pants were chafing my thighs, I had to get back into vacation mode and return to my objective, making love to as many beautiful prostitutes as I could in the remaining five days of my visit to Rio. Before saying goodbye to my fashion consultant, I left her some extra *reality* to have my seersucker pants dry-cleaned. She informed me that the dry-cleaning wouldn't be ready until Friday.

"Friday!" I exclaimed. "I'm leaving Saturday. Can't I pay extra for next-day service?" Tiffany explained that Rio was not New York and that things moved at a much slower pace since people spent so much of their time making love. I offered to give her enough money to cover a motivational blowjob for the dry-cleaner, but she wasn't sure the incentive would guarantee next-day service. Blowjobs, which were a dime-a-dozen in Rio, had lost their value as persuasive currency for most locals.

Tiffany had wanted me to trade my bowtie and jacket for one of those tight-fitting tropical shirts worn open at the neck, but

I didn't have any gold chains and I wasn't sure it was the right look for me. My mother had always stressed the importance of dressing for success and looking like a gentleman, and I didn't feel comfortable when I wasn't wearing the bowtie that had become my calling card. Besides, if I dressed in typical Rio attire, I would just look like everyone else.

Rolling her eyes at my obstinacy, Tiffany pointed me in the direction of The Catwalk, which wasn't far away, telling me that once I got there, any of the girls would be able to tell me how to get to The Gringo.

It occurred to me that I hadn't seen a live vagina in almost 18 hours, having gotten waylaid at The Club House and then pinned to the ground by an Amazonian Jiu-Jitsu master. My heart was pounding in my chest as I started to make my way toward The Catwalk. I couldn't imagine what it would be like to be confronted with so many vaginas all at once. I have heard that blind people who get their sight back often suffer from a condition called agnosia, in which they can't recognize common objects. I was worried that I had been so deprived of the sight of naked women that I might not be able to tell one vagina from another. In New York, unlike Rio, only about twenty-five percent of the female population become prostitutes. And many of those don't even realize their true calling. They simply end up marrying men they don't love just for the money, and once they get the hang of it they tend to do the same thing over and over. Some people just call that being married more than once, but I believe it describes a woman who has chosen a life of prostitution.

My new pair of pants was definitely a double-edged sword. If I made it as far as The Catwalk, I would very likely meet more prostitutes, but I began to doubt that I would be able to do anything about it if circulation to my crotch was cut off. All through childhood I had heard stories about men losing their testicles due to untreated hernias. Risky as it was, I decided it made more sense to jettison the pants and just show up at The Catwalk in my new bikini briefs. In this case, my mother's instruction to always wear a tie came to the rescue. No one could accuse me of being inappropriately dressed. Even without pants, I wasn't going to be turned away from a nightclub if I was wearing a jacket and tie. Besides, this was a tropical climate where it wasn't unusual to wear shorts even for the most formal get-togethers. If anyone asked about my thong, I'd tell them I was on my way to a midnight shark hunt and that it was just a bathing suit.

Finally, in the distance, I saw what looked like a totally naked woman standing under a canopy. The only items of clothing she seemed to be wearing were a baseball cap and stiletto heels. As I watched her take a set of keys from the driver of a cherry-red Porsche and execute a flawless three-point turn into a tight spot further down the street, I realized she was the valet. I wouldn't need to ask her if I could see her vagina, since even from a distance it was plainly visible. I could also see that she was an old-school girl who didn't shave her thick muff. I'd heard about Brazilian hot waxing, and it was the one thing that had almost made me decide to change my vacation plans, as the trend toward clean shaving struck me as a form of collective pedophilia.

I licked my lips as I approached the little velvet rope that was presided over by a trio of imposing bouncers. I noticed that neither the bouncers nor the nude valet seemed to pay the least attention to me.

Figuring that I didn't know the customs, I proceeded to unlatch the velvet rope myself. Suddenly I felt a hand clamping down on my shoulder. "It's closed for a private party," one of the bouncers said. As before, I wondered how so many of the natives knew to address me in English, but it was neither the time nor the place to linger on such details. Other men, whose cars were parked by the naked valet, walked right past me and were ushered to the gates of heaven unimpeded. When I tried to point out this inconsistency in the admissions policy, I was simply told, "We cannot accommodate your party tonight." I didn't understand. This was Rio, where everything was supposed to be free and open. Yet I was blocked by a velvet rope like I was at Studio 54 in its '70s heyday.

During a slight lull in the traffic, the naked valet came over to me. She rubbed her thumb and fingers together to remind me that a little *reality* was more persuasive than words. Obviously, I was thinking too analytically about something that required a simple solution. I waved one of the bouncers over and, just as he was about to shoo me off with another "I can't accommodate your party," reached out my hand, proffering a 100 *real* note. The change in his attitude was dramatic. Suddenly, I was treated like a long-lost friend and ushered into the club, where a bevy of beautiful Tiffanys with gigantic breasts and uncharacteristically big bushes sat me down at a VIP table and started asking challenging questions like, "Can I blow you?" and "Do you want to fuck?" They were all so alluring I didn't know what to do, or with whom. I decided that since I'd waited this long, I was going to savor the moment and delay gratification. I didn't want to use up all my juice before the evening ended. If the girls at The Catwalk were this enticing and willing, there was no telling what bounty The Gringo would hold.

Where all doors had seemed closed to me, in an instant the world was my oyster. The Catwalk was designed like a theater in the round. There was a stage about which phalanxes of naked girls, whose faces were made up to look like pussy cats and whose vaginas looked like beavers lolling in a pond, paraded wantonly every half-hour or so. The atmosphere had the flavor of a disco, circa 1977, which may have explained the marked absence amongst the denizens of waxing or shaving. The grooming, as I would later learn, reflected the segment of Brazilian society that still held on to the all-natural fashion sensibility of a bygone era.

The entire seating area was in shadow, with lots of private

crannies, where I noticed figures engaging in a variety of sexual acts. I'd once been in a restaurant in Hong Kong where the room seemed to be swaying like the car on a Ferris wheel, and when I sat down at my table I realized the floor was covered with snakes, which were cooked in little pots in front of the diners. The floor of The Catwalk reminded me of that restaurant, except the snakes were replaced by writhing, naked bodies. I felt dizzy until I realized there was an orgy taking place at my feet. Girls whose heads weren't bobbing up and down in acts of fellatio were on the floor performing sixty-nine with each other, or with anyone who was interested and could afford to pay for it.

I soon realized I had made a mistake in jettisoning my tight jeans, since I had a tremendous hard-on that wouldn't go away, no matter what profoundly asexual thoughts I tried to conjure. Though Manhattan isn't Rio, the first days of spring usually bring an onslaught of women in revealing attire, and when I get hard in a crowded subway or bus after unavoidably rubbing up against a woman, I think about the Holocaust. I'm Jewish, so I feel little guilt about appropriating images from the concentration camps for my own dubious purposes. But in my present straits, none of the usual tricks seemed to be working, and there was nothing I could do to camouflage my condition. I realized I was in danger of being raped. All a Tiffany would have to do is sit on me. I decided that the best thing I could do was to keep in motion until I found the Tiffany I was looking for. So I took to the dance floor, where the blaring classic '70s disco beats of Donna Summer and the Bee Gees had given way to the soft merengue of "Push Push in the Bush." I have never had any problem dancing by myself. In fact I frequently dance in front of the full-length mirror on my closet door at home, pretending I'm a rock star should a song like Rod Stewart's "Baby Jane" come on the radio. In this case I just had to be sure to keep a substantial distance between myself and anyone else, and above all avoid poking the other dancers with my stiff prick.

The mix of naked, pheromone-producing bodies must have acted like a drug, because I wound up doing the macarena with a small dark-haired woman. She had big almond-shaped eyes that looked like they were constantly welling up with tears. I thought she was crying because she didn't like being paraded around in front of a group of men whose collective horniness had been provoked to the point of histrionic frenzy. Perhaps she was one of those women who had been lured into a sub-prime mortgage and now had to sell her body to avoid foreclosure.

Later I would learn that the name of the girl I was dancing with was, in fact, Tiffany. She had hypnotized me, and when I came out of my trance I realized that she had inordinately huge, perfect breasts and a virtual forest between her legs. I was eager to explore my newfound friend with both my fingers and my tongue, but something was holding me back. Tiffany seemed like relationship material, one of those complex hookers who brought a lot of emotional baggage along with her sexual allure, and I didn't want to get emotionally involved with someone at The Catwalk before I'd even made it to The Gringo. I had gotten into a serious relationship with a hooker during my first year at Columbia and ended up regretting the loss of my youthful opportunity to play the field.

As I felt her furry vagina rubbing up against my hardened penis, I let my hands wander over her velvety folds, finally letting my fingers crawl inside of her like little snakes ferreting out their prey. She was impassive in the face of my prying, which was now taking on the quality of an exuberant gynecological exam. I love touching vaginas so much that I had once toyed around with the notion of becoming a gynecologist. However, my mother's own excitement about the prospects of my being a doctor blunted my ambitions. Every time I thought about a woman in stirrups, I saw my mother's face. She was understandably disappointed when I dropped the idea. In her inimitable way she would ask, "You're going to make your own mother pay to have some stranger examine her?" I dropped organic biology and majored in economics precisely to avoid such potentially embarrassing Oedipal scenes.

Tiffany kept staring at me like a long-lost lover, and I began to wonder if indeed I'd met her somewhere else, even in another life. I'm a firm believer in the transmigration of souls, and it seemed reasonable that I could purchase her services even if her body was occupied by another spirit. When she looked at me with those doe eyes and asked if I wanted a blowjob, I told her we'd better talk first. I knew that acknowledging the depths of Tiffany's feelings was a potential rabbit hole. The question of emotional intimacy was in fact a point that I wanted to bring up with my psychoanalyst friends at the hotel, because I was beginning to get the sneaking suspicion that free will might be playing a greater role in human affairs than Freud had accounted for. For instance, I had the choice to behave like an animal and accept the blowjob, or, like Hamlet, to deliberate before doing anything rash. I readily accepted the fact that it might turn out that behaving like an animal with Tiffany was the humane thing to do. On the other hand, getting involved with her complex problems and psychohistory as an excuse for getting into her pants set up expectations I could never fulfill.

Still, the side of me that leans toward relationship-building with whores was winning out again. I led Tiffany over to the quietest little nook I could find, where another couple was already engaged in an unclassifiable sex act, and asked her if she wanted to talk about anything. I ordered a couple of margaritas.

The old expression "you can't see the forest for the trees" certainly proved true in our case, since my ability to listen to what Tiffany was actually saying was impeded by the fact that I couldn't take my eyes off the extraordinary flora and fauna between her legs. Tiffany spoke excellent English and, from what I could tell, American intellectuals like Susan Sontag must have been quite a craze among the prostitutes of Brazil, because

Tiffany, like her older predecessor, turned out to be extremely knowledgeable about Sontag's work. In fact, she owned an autographed copy of the Portuguese version of *Against Interpretation.*

As it happened, her slide into a life of prostitution had nothing to do with poverty or lack of education, but rather an over-immersion in the work of the French deconstructionists, particularly Derrida, whose writing she had interpreted in an overly literal way. She had initially gone into therapy to palliate her inability to think metaphorically, but over the years, as she moved into regular, four-day-a-week analysis, the work concentrated more on her idealization of the French intellectuals. She didn't turn tricks for the money, since her father was a wealthy industrialist, but more as a constant reminder that she was part of a barter economy in which sex was a commodity like anything else. Besides, she enjoyed taking her clothes off in front of strange men.

As she continued to unspool her life's story, Tiffany's left nipple nestled into the center of her margarita and floated there like an olive in a martini. She was getting very emotional and I realized that it might become increasingly difficult to segue into a sex act. I couldn't imagine interrupting her tale to ask if she could take my penis in her mouth. How would she ever be able to get to the denouement?

My heart skipped a beat, however, and my fears were assuaged when Tiffany interrupted her own account by getting up from the table, standing in front of me with her big hairy pussy in my face, and announcing, "I have to pee. Why don't we go back to my father's place? He has a huge mansion in a small town on the coast just outside Rio." I was about to admit to her that I hadn't bothered to rent a car since the hotel provided free shuttle service when she announced, "We can zoom up there in my Alfa."

I noticed that she still hadn't put any clothes on as the valet pulled her car up to the door of the club. I did think it was odd, but I rationalized that perhaps in Rio it was common for the beautiful daughters of wealthy industrialists to drive their fancy sports cars in the nude. As we drove through downtown Rio with the top down and the windows open, I remarked that none of the other drivers even blinked at the sight of a nude Tiffany passing them in traffic. This would never go over on the Long Island Expressway, where she would certainly have caused one of the greatest pileups in transportation history.

I was beginning to notice that she remained curiously incurious about me. She just stared at the road with her dark, brooding eyes as she talked. It was apparent that she was a true narcissist whose seeming attention-giving was only a subterfuge by which she could call attention to herself.

As we swung out onto the majestic coastal road leading out of Rio, past the sparkling beaches crowded with Tiffanys plying their trade late into the night, Tiffany's nipples hardened as she continued to tell me her saga.

Her father had wanted her older brother to take over the family empire, which included considerable real estate holdings. But the brother wanted to be a poet and had moved to Paris, where he tried his hand at writing while living off the earnings of his wife, a very successful prostitute in the Pigalle. They had two daughters who would undoubtedly follow in their mother's footsteps. She told me that most of her brother's poems were about his hatred for their father and that, with the French economy being in the state it was, it was likely that his teenage daughters would do much better selling their bodies than trying to sell the kind of poetry their father was churning out. The bitter irony was that both girls were artistically inclined and dreamt of being famous writers who could one day produce the same kind of hate-filled screeds as their dad.

As we drove along, with the moonlight shining over the cresting waves of the Atlantic, I began to panic. I was on my way to the auspicious residence of a major Brazilian industrialist, and though I was wearing a Brooks Brothers seersucker jacket, bow-tie, and preppy white dress shirt, I still didn't have any pants. Even though Tiffany was totally nude, I didn't know the mores of the society I was entering. Perhaps before she walked into her childhood home, Tiffany would pull a shift out of the trunk, maybe a servant would come running out to her with a bathing suit and robe so she could jump into a topiary-surrounded pool for a midnight swim, while I stood around awkwardly trying to cover myself. I needed to achieve a level of comfort. I asked Tiffany if there was somewhere we could stop so that I could buy some pants. Tiffany laughed like one of the insouciant vamps in early Italian neorealist cinema. "Your pants are what I like to do without, baby," Tiffany giggled. Then she let out a whoop and floored the accelerator around a blind curve leading up a mountain pass.

A large oil truck happened to be coming right at us as we rounded the turn. For a moment, I was sure I was going to meet my maker, so I closed my eyes and thanked God that at least I would die next to a beautiful, aristocratic Tiffany who far exceeded even my wildest imaginings. I love psychoanalysis, but I'm also an aficionado of modern drama, and my life was beginning to remind me of Strindberg's *A Dream Play*. I couldn't tell the curves of the body undulating next to me from the curves in the treacherous mountain road that we were climbing. It was a curious medley of emotions, a mixture of joy and terrible fear.

I almost lost my breath when we pulled up in front of two huge gates guarded by naked Valkyries who had Uzis strapped over their shoulders in a way that barely obscured their breasts. The only uniforms they were wearing were stiletto high heels and the kind of officer's hats worn by The Village People. Both of the guards had big hairy bushes that made my mouth water. I was reminded of Castro's guerillas, who had distinguished themselves with their fulsome beards.

"Are they whores too?" I asked.

"Sure, everybody who works for us is."

It turned out her mother, Tiffany, was one of Brazil's most venerated whores. She was of mixed ancestry, representing the wedding of two distinguished family lines. Tiffany's grandmother had been a famous Amazonian princess whose legendary sexual abilities were documented in the Brazilian equivalent of the *Kama Sutra*. She'd married a Portuguese general who'd achieved notoriety for his conquests both on land and in bed. Tiffany told me that when her mother was making her way as a famous prostitute, she slept with a majority of the members of both houses of Brazil's parliament, making her the most powerful woman in the country, at least while congress was in session. Even though she was a known prostitute, her beauty was such that she constantly received marriage proposals from some of the most renowned figures in politics and the arts, but she had turned them all down in favor of living the life of whoredom that she loved. It was only when she was well past her prime that she'd finally settled down with one of her best customers.

Despite Tiffany's torrid past, I wanted to make sure that before I paid for sex I'd succeeded in creating a meaningful relationship between us. Anyone can pay for sex, but it's the rare john who can create a bond based on respect, dignity, and shared goals.

I had never met the parents of any of the whores I'd fucked over the years. I felt that the opportunity to meet Tiffany's parents was a privilege that could only increase our intimacy. Tiffany had revealed herself to me, in that she had been nude from the moment I met her, but this was a chance to really get to know the person beneath the beautiful breasts and outspoken Venus mound. I was going to be humping a woman whose history was now an open book to me, just like her genitalia. In the past, I would pay for sex and only afterward, sated and proud of my monstrous capacity, would I indifferently begin to ask a few probing questions. Conversation was exactly like fucking. When

I paid for a woman, I could do anything I wanted to her, and our post-coital repartee was just an extension of my desire to explore. I would ask how many men she had screwed that day, how she had gotten into the life, and even what she did about her periods.

The mansion was situated atop a huge piece of rock and surrounded by gardens. Tiffany entered a security code and an electric gate opened. We drove to the end of a long gravel driveway that led to the entrance of the stucco-walled mansion itself. There was a strong Oriental influence in the structure, which was like an enormous pagoda covered with an elaborate tile roof. Despite the guards all around, there was an air of total freedom, as the doors to the rooms (including bathrooms) were all open. I no sooner walked in than I passed a bedroom where a couple was involved in an act of vigorous missionary sex. There was a winding marble staircase, which reminded me of *Auntie Mame*, especially when Tiffany called out what I took to be the equivalent of "Hi, Mom" in Portuguese and a stunning creature wearing a long, open silk robe descended the stairs to greet us. I loved Tiffany, but when I saw the mound between her mother's legs, which actually looked like a raccoon, I knew I was in real trouble. If there is a psychoanalytic term for the desire for the mother of a woman you want to fuck, I was suffering from it. I should have seen the writing on the wall, but I wasn't looking at a wall when Tiffany's mother held out her hand.

"Kenny Cantor," I said taking her hand into mine.

"Tiffany" she replied in a matter-of-fact tone that acknowledged the provenance of her name. Her breasts touched against my seersucker jacket as she kissed me on both cheeks in the European style. Her name was actually Tiffany de Los Santos Salazar. "I've heard so much about you. I'm looking forward to fucking you later," she purred.

I wasn't sure how she could have heard about me, but in the age of high-speed Internet and the Blackberry, anything was possible. I had noticed that Brazilians texted almost as much as they fucked. I also realized that from a psychoanalytic point of view the situation in Tiffany's house conformed to neither the classical Oedipal nor interpersonal models, and that I might need a more cutting edge approach in order to understand the relationships within the family.

"Tiffany, your father wants to see you before dinner."

"He probably just wants a blowjob," she giggled.

The nudity and intergenerational fucking were surprising—all the more so since, glancing at my watch, I realized it was three in the morning. Like all college kids, I went out for hamburgers or pizza after late-night parties, but in Tiffany's family everyone dressed up for dinner in the wee hours of the morning. In fact it was the only time they dressed. Like Jews who recline at Passover, by the end of the meal the women had their slinky dresses pulled up to their navels so they were ready for the obligatory tango that followed all major meals. That was in fact how Tiffany and I almost consummated our relationship. We were dancing closely in a style that used to be called The Grind when I was in high school, and Tiffany simply reached into my little bikini underwear and stuck my penis into her. It didn't take much since my erection had been growing ever since the meal ended, and she lazily began to pull her elegant gown up to reveal her fury cunt, which I had nicknamed Che (after Che Guevara), but just as I was about to come, my eyes locked with her father's and I lost my erection.

The short-circuiting was so overwhelming to my senses that it must have eradicated some of the mnemonic pathways between the hippocampus and the prefrontal cortex. I'm a bit of a heretic when it comes to orgasm, which I believe has transcendent and even religious facets that divorce it from the vicissitudes of the conflicts that preoccupy psychoanalysts, so I was surprised by the failure I was experiencing.

Despite the disorientation created by the blockage of my

own energies, I noticed that Tiffany's mother was dancing with one of the waiters who had served dinner. I couldn't help associating her hairy pussy with the hairstyles of geniuses like Mozart, Beethoven, and Einstein. Tiffany's father was already getting blown and rimmed by two of the pool attendants. I had felt a little self-conscious when Tiffany pulled her dress up and started to dance with me right in front of him, but after we were done dancing and had returned to the table for coffee, dessert, and aperitifs, he seemed totally unruffled by the fact that I had just tried to fuck his daughter.

I noted almost immediately that possessiveness and jealousy were absent in this household. Here was a family unit seemingly devoid of any rivalry or generational antipathy. It reminded me of the Sullivanians back in Manhattan, who had attempted to break down some of the patterns of Oedipal conflict by abolishing exclusivity in sexual relationships.

Tiffany's parents' home was like an old-fashioned hippie commune, except that it managed to maintain all the trappings—fancy cars, gardeners, pool attendants, servants, and security guards—of aristocratic society. I realized that servant girls getting fucked by the master was no real advance in civilization, since it practically defined the master-servant relationship throughout history, but, outside of the Marquis de Sade, I hadn't heard of any aristocratic manses where everyone was on such an equal footing.

I didn't know if I was falling in love with Tiffany or her family's way of life. My own family had had a Russian cleaning woman who came to our Kew Gardens apartment once a week, but she was hardly the kind of woman you wanted to see without her headscarf, much less in the nude. I came from a totally middle-class background, which exuded none of the glamour of Tiffany's aristocratic forbears. My parents mostly sat in front of the television watching Milton Berle and Lawrence Welk, drinking tea and rooting among the chocolates in the thick Barricini boxes for the ones that had the caramel or nougat centers.

I knew that Brazilians, like many Latin peoples, liked to eat late, but dessert didn't end until dawn and had many courses of its own, including a segment in which naked Amazonian women with unusually large secondary sex characteristics passed out *digestifs* and played the bongos. I noticed that whenever I started to make romantic gestures toward Tiffany, she quickly suggested an activity that was more appropriate to a hooker. When I tried to kiss her, she immediately asked me if I wanted her to go down on me. When I took her hand, she wanted to know if I wanted to finger-fuck her, at one point offering, "You can do me in the ass, if you like."

While at first I was afraid that I was getting so exclusively involved with Tiffany that I wouldn't be able to play the field and meet other eligible whores at The Gringo, I now started to imagine all kinds of scenes of domestic bliss with her. Now that I am thinking about it, I realize that my desire was predicated on impossibility. The only reason I let myself want Tiffany was because I realized I couldn't have her.

Still, I couldn't stop marveling at her crotch, and I imagined that hairy bush lying next to me every night, offering me solace like my old dog, whose furry snout was always within reach. I imagined living on this Edenic estate, where I now felt like little more than an interloper. Of course we would acquire an estate of our own, overlooking the beach at Ipanema, saving money by wisely managing and investing Tiffany's earnings. I would add to the pot by doing a little tax work of my own on the side. I'd pay homage to Tiffany's great grandmother by playing old Stan Getz albums. I allowed myself the luxury of imagining a whole family. I would ensure Tiffany's legacy by fathering a whole line of daughters, talented whores in their own right, who would proudly parade their pudenda in the family name.

I knew in my heart that Tiffany, however introspective she

was for a whore, however deep her perceptions and however articulate she could be, even with my penis in her mouth, was basically one of those girls who just wanted to have fun. I realized my possessive attitude toward Tiffany would get me into a lot of trouble with my Sullivanian psychoanalyst friends back in New York, and that my delusions and desires would make it increasingly difficult to take a realistic attitude about the rest of my vacation.

I began to think that I should call the hotel and try to speak to China, or even the great Schmucker himself. On the other hand, Schmucker, though known for his insights, was not known for his empathy. Legend had it that he had once told a patient that if he needed support, he should get a jockstrap. I'd caught a glimpse of him giving a presentation in another room as I left Sunshine's lecture, and he talked about the human psyche the way a drill sergeant speaks to his men before an engagement. In fact, his account of one of his cases reminded me of a Pentagon briefing by the Joint Chiefs of Staff after a bombing in Iraq, and when he'd finished it sounded much like George Bush's fateful "mission accomplished." Even though Schmucker kept repeating the Freudian mantra that there were no easy answers and that everything was over-determined, he was plainly trying to persuade his audience that he really did have the answers. I was afraid that even if I managed to find the courage to wake him in the early morning hours and negotiate a fee, he would just tell me I had to leave Tiffany if I wanted to achieve a happy life with a hooker. The other thing I realized was that Tiffany, for all her aristocratic upbringing, was neither a happy camper nor a carefree hooker. I had known that from the first moment I looked down into her crotch, and then up into her eyes to see that she was crying. I started to wonder if my cock had not become to her what a pacifier is to a baby. Perhaps constantly putting cocks in her mouth every time she felt sad was a way of running away from her fears.

All these thoughts were running through my head as I watched the sun rise over the distant *favelas* of Rio. I was becoming more and more involved with perhaps one of the most mysteriously alluring Tiffanys I'd ever encountered. We had now been together longer than I had ever been with a prostitute, and all she did when she wasn't dancing naked or trying to fulfill my sexual urges was cry. I tried to take the analytic attitude of a listener, keeping a poker face while at the same time making terse editorial comments aimed at getting her to talk about some of the feelings that were coming up. Inevitably, I ended up popping out with some of the typical shibboleths of analysis: "Do I remind you of your father?" and "Is my interest in you perhaps causing some discomfort?" Considering my own dysfunction, I might have asked myself if her father reminded me of my own, but comparisons between the Brazilian industrialist and the middle-class Jew from Queens simply fell flat.

I asked her if she realized that there were women who were not prostitutes and, based on her response, I could tell it was something she really hadn't thought about. Her mother, grandmother, and great-grandmother had all been well-known Brazilian whores. All the rest of the women in her family were whores, as were all her friends, and naturally all the female employees in her father's factories and on his estate. Prostitution was the only life she had known. I was beginning to think that the problem, in some regard, was me, and that it went back to the first time she'd seen me strutting around The Catwalk in my bikini underwear. Perhaps she'd realized I was relationship material, while at the same time not having the awareness to deal with the emotions that her attraction to me was eliciting.

As the night ended, and I went so far as to imagine us trying to get our kids into Manhattan private schools, I began to suspect that she was picking up on my distinctly domestic fantasies and wishes, while at the same time finding them hard to process.

Even Brazilians have to stop dancing and eating and having

sex so they can get some sleep, and when the sun started to assert itself as more than a decorative presence, rising over the Atlantic, beating down on us as we swayed to a morning mambo, the true nature of my predicament stared me right in the face. Though paying Tiffany would be no problem (I had plenty of *reals* on me), I had no way of getting back to my hotel, even if I wanted to, and I didn't have any pants. As trivial as it may sound in a liberated society where nudity is rampant, I was still a Manhattanite at heart, and felt uncomfortable walking through a hotel lobby in my underpants. Indeed, I hadn't noticed any Brazilians parading around the hotel in my state of undress. It was one thing to be naked on a beach or in somebody's *hacienda* or even, like Tiffany, cruising around in a sports car. It was another to waltz up in one's underwear to the concierge at a hotel, where a certain degree of formality and decorum were required. In addition, what if I were to walk into the lobby of the hotel and run into Herbert Schmucker or China Dentata?

I noticed that Tiffany had fallen asleep on a chaise longue, and for a moment I worried that she might get a sunburn on her pussy and not be able to perform her professional duties. But I assumed that her dark complexion enabled her to absorb sunlight better than a North American like myself. I hate to wake up a sleeping hooker. It is so rare that prostitutes get to sleep while on the job, and I felt the level of trust that had been building up between Tiffany and me was something that had to be cherished and cultivated, especially if we were to create a life together and become the top horses in each other's stables.

There were so many unresolved questions. I had to get back to the hotel and into psychoanalysis, if only for a few days, while Schmucker and China were still in town. With all my experience, I knew that psychoanalysis was not like the trauma therapy they give to the survivors of plane accidents, earthquakes, and hurricanes. I was aware that it was a slow, laborious process that went on for years. But Lacan had revolutionized analytic treatment with his short sessions that sometimes lasted no more than a minute, and for which the patient still paid for his full hour. I saw no reason why I couldn't pay some outrageous fee to be psychoanalyzed in the three remaining days of my vacation. Psychoanalysis wasn't part of my original package, which included airfare, deluxe hotel accommodation, and continental breakfast, but with the psychoanalytic conventioneers occupying so many rooms at the hotel, I knew there must be plans that offered therapy, as well as sex, as part of a package.

I hadn't paid Tiffany a cent, but I figured she was running a tab and that when we were done she would present me with a bill for the numerous blowjobs she had tried to give me, as well as for the failed fuck while we had been dancing. It wasn't as if these were tax-deductible items that needed to be itemized, but I'm an accountant, so I like to know what I'm paying for.

I whispered softly into Tiffany's ear, asking her if there were any buses that could take me back to the hotel. "Don't you want to try to stick it in again?" she murmured, pulling my prick out of my bikini briefs and holding it in her mouth like one of those cigars that Fidel Castro used to puff on.

"I think we need to talk."

"Okay, let's talk," she moaned as she filled her mouth with me.

"I want to end the relationship." The words came out of my mouth involuntarily and I wanted to take them back immediately. Tiffany took my penis out of her mouth for a moment, holding it in her hand as if she were the master of ceremonies at the mic, about to toast the bar mitzvah boy. Without making any pronouncements, she started sliding it in and out of her mouth vigorously. I guess she felt she could suck my feelings away. Perhaps she thought she could blow my brains out. This had occurred at several moments in my adult sex life, when an orgasm was so overpowering that it essentially became an out-of-body experience. I think she had the idea that she was so good with her mouth that she could use it to eliminate any of the doubts I might have had in my head.

I don't think I'd ever tried to come so many times in one twenty-four-hour period, all unsuccessfully, and I couldn't remember ever getting so close to a hooker as I had to Tiffany. But I didn't lose my resolve.

"You're a beautiful, young woman with a lot going for you. But I'm not ready to settle down and spend the rest of my vacation with the same woman, no matter how expensive her services are. I still haven't even set foot in The Gringo. I feel like I would be doing myself a disservice."

"The Gringo is just filled with whores," she said.

We just looked at each other with the resignation that a couple has when something painful yet very true comes out in a counseling session or a conversation. I couldn't believe what was happening, and I was filled with doubt, but I also shored myself up and adopted a steely determination. I would have put my pants on if I had any.

A few minutes later I was standing at the bus stop below the cliff that faced the mountainous estate, which looked dramatically out over a pristine ocean vista. The whole scene was Jane Eyre in reverse. Tiffany was the tormented Rochester in his aerie. I was the innocent Jane, forced to rely on reason and old-fashioned common sense to survive in a sea of overwhelming emotions. As much as I longed to return to the estate's hallowed halls and lay my eyes on Tiffany's operatic Venus mound, making love beneath the portraits of the great whores and sluts of her aristocratic ancestry, I knew I had to break away from a relationship that was doomed from the start.

The buses coming down into Rio from the mountains are supposed to follow a schedule, but despite very different topography they behaved similarly to the buses on Fifth Avenue, which come in herds and then disappear completely for long stretches of time. I wasn't sure what bus to take, and I didn't have the Brazilian equivalent of a MetroCard, but I had the kind of *reality* that could get me anywhere. Hanging around at Tiffany's parents' estate, I was at the top of the economic ladder. Brazil is still a third-world country with a huge population living in shacks and shantytowns, and if 150 *reals* will buy a 69 from nobility like Tiffany, it wasn't hard to imagine what the Tiffanys of the peasant class would do for even less. Hitching a ride back to Rio for the same amount seemed like a more than reasonable expectation.

A crowd of leathery peasant women in muslin dresses, their hair wrapped in scarves, suddenly surrounded me. Perhaps it was the bikini underwear. I immediately asked which way to the Copacabana. One of them must have understood me since she pulled out a piece of paper and pencil and started to draw a little map of the Rio shoreline. Unable to decipher her crude map, I immediately asked if any of them had a global positioning device, calling out the letters "GPS" to make my point. They couldn't figure out what I was talking about and they turned their attentions back to the heavy burlap bags filled with produce they were readying themselves to heft. Soon a bus rounded a sharp curve, bearing down on us at such a high rate of speed that it looked like the centrifugal force was going to cause it to careen off the side of the cliff. But the old hags had their eyes on something else, pointing excitedly toward the gardens at the back of the huge estate, their toothless mouths gaping with screams of delight. Looking up, I glimpsed Tiffany's father's infamous gang of naked gardeners, their personal topiaries glistening in the morning dew. Before following my fellow travelers onto the rickety bus, I noticed that its luggage rack was piled high with suitcases and boxes, which looked perilously in danger of either falling off or causing the bus to topple on its side.

As we moved toward the center of the city and then out toward the Copacabana, I noticed that even though it was early morning, the streets were filled with hookers, who I assumed were just coming to the end of the late shift. There was only one time of day when it was really hard to get a hooker in Rio, and that was from mid-morning to early afternoon, when the night shift had already gone home and the girls who worked from 4 p.m. to midnight had yet to punch the clock. It was like in New York, where it's impossible to get a cab between three and five in the afternoon, when the night men have yet to come on. The only difference was that hookers in Rio didn't have off-duty signs to turn on like taxis.

To my relief, I wasn't the only person in the lobby walking around in his underwear. In fact, men clad in boxers, briefs, or old-style Jockey underpants, of the kind my mother used to buy three-for-$5 at Woolworths, outnumbered those dressed in normal street clothes. It was apparent to me that most of the men, tourists like myself, were still in somewhat of a daze, undoubtedly having experienced one of the best nights of their lives. I walked over to the auditorium where the analytic conference was set to convene to check into that day's presentation.

The lecture of the day was on "Erotomania," a condition also referred to as De Clerambault's Syndrome, in which a person has the delusion that they are desired by a well-known figure who doesn't even know they exist. Before I'd left for Rio, the case of Uma Thurman's stalker had been in the headlines, and when I'd read the accounts I considered the possibility that the stalker was actually in the right, that Uma was really in love with him but just didn't know it. Being reminded of this made me question my whole night with Tiffany. Maybe I was just another john to her. Maybe I was investing a tremendous amount of emotional energy in someone who didn't even fully grasp my existence. Maybe the guilt I felt about breaking away from her was a figment of my imagination.

I also had forebodings about Schmucker and China Dentata. They met so many people—would they even remember me? In addition, I was feeling the stress typical of anyone at a psychoanalytic conference who wants to make time for sight-seeing, although in my case the sights were the accoutrements of local streetwalkers. How could I attend the lecture on ero-tomania, get some sleep, get laid, and also have time to termi-nate an analysis I had yet to begin? Analyses go on for years, but there is no time limit and no strict rules, especially since the Lacanians had shown that sessions didn't have to conform to the 50-minute model, and could be as short as one minute in duration. There are 60 minutes in an hour. If I devoted 60 of my remaining 96 hours in Rio to analysis, I could have the equivalent of 3,600 Lacanian sessions, based on the one-minute model. The typical patient, who sees an analyst four days per week for approximately 48 weeks of the year (since most ana-lysts take August off), only does 192 sessions in a year. So by my calculations I would be able to undergo the equivalent of almost 19 years of analysis in roughly four days, simply by shortening my sessions to the absolute minimum allowed by the academy that regulates Lacanian analysis.

With regards to China, there was something more global that I didn't even want to think about. It related to the compromise of her analytic neutrality. I was starting to veer into a series of thoughts typical of most patients—thoughts that led to the in-evitable desire to sleep with one's analyst. In my case, the fan-tasy was complicated by the fact that I wanted to sleep with an analyst with whom I hadn't even begun treatment. I wasn't sure if the transference with China could be called positive or not.

When I crossed the lobby, I could see China sitting in the breakfast nook of one of the hotel's restaurants, auspiciously named The New Yorker. I could see the back of the head of the older man she was talking to, and even though I had never stud-ied phrenology, I was sure it was Schmucker. I was seized by a murderous jealousy that almost made it impossible for me to sit down and have a little breakfast of my own. I was afraid to look, afraid that the emotions of seeing Schmucker and China, who I now began to suspect were lovers, would provoke in me an impulse-control problem with grave repercussions. Still, I put one foot in front of the other and headed for a long table covered with bowls of stewed fruits, plates of pastries and croissants, and platters of cheese and cold cuts. Sitting down at a table, my legs shaking with agitation, I was surprised that I had the wherewithal to ask the beautiful, young waitress, who was wearing a nameplate on the breast pocket of her uniform that read "Tiffany," if I might obtain an omelet to anchor my breakfast. Tiffany was playing with her skirt, and she picked it up enough to reveal the little pink fold that gave away the fact that she wasn't wearing any underwear. I noticed a banana nestled in her apron pocket in a suggestive way that only Brazilian waitresses knew how to pull off. Even fruits had lost their innocence in this Garden of Eden. She pulled the banana out, rubbing it against her elegant neck and then rolling it across her lips.

"We have some very nice bananas," she said. "They're still green, but when you take them back to your room they get ripe."

I was about to go into analysis, where it's recommended that patients avoid any major life changes for at least the first year, which according to my calculations meant I shouldn't start seeing any new Brazilian whores for at least another 3 hours and 12 minutes. Of course, who knew when that would be, seeing that I hadn't talked to China or Schmucker about starting treatment. But how was I going to explain this to my beautiful banana-wielding Tiffany? Clearly, a woman so charmingly unperturbed by the social conventions of underwear could hardly be expected to understand the exigencies of Lacanian analysis. If I told her I was going to have 3,600 one-minute sessions, translating into the equivalent of 19 years of therapy in the remaining 96 hours I was in Rio, she would undoubtedly think I was nuts. Long-term therapy has always been hard to explain in modern times, with our need for quick fixes and painless remedies, and Brazilian society is no exception. I wouldn't have known where to begin when it came to explaining something like Lacanian analysis, in which a therapeutic interaction that only lasts a minute costs as much as a one-hour session.

The sole thing I was capable of blurting out was, "That banana really looks hard!" to which Tiffany replied with a tantalizing, "Ooooh," shaking her bum at me as she sashayed over to the table occupied by China. Schmucker had signaled to the waitress for the bill in the impatient manner typical of New Yorkers. For a moment I mused on the differences between Brazilian waitresses and their counterparts in the States. To begin with, relatively few waitresses who work the dining rooms of luxury hotels in the States are hookers, although they might as well be, considering how they debase themselves for a good tip. Secondly, few waitresses I had met would have chosen to use a name like Tiffany during working hours (even if it was their given name), and fewer still would have stuck bananas in their uniform pockets in Tiffany's suggestive manner.

I felt a moment of yearning, but I also realized that I had to seize an important opportunity to get the help I needed. Once the talk on erotomania started, both China and Schmucker would become absorbed in the presentation, and even though I might get into an academic discussion with them, it would be hard to shift the conversation to my personal sufferings. It was now or never.

I drifted over to the table where Schmucker and China were seated and was lurking behind Schmucker, hoping he wouldn't notice me approaching. It was only when China slunk back into her seat and asked Schmucker, "How much do I owe you?" that she noticed me and exclaimed, "Dr. Cantor!"

For a moment I wasn't going to say anything. After all, my mother had always wanted me to be a doctor. But I realized that with time being so short, it made no sense for my therapeutic progress to perpetuate a lie.

"I'm not an analyst. I'm not even a doctor. But I need one."

I tend to be a macho male when it comes to making myself vulnerable or expressing emotion. But all of a sudden I was overcome both with tears and a countervailing feeling of total humiliation. Walking around in my underwear might have been mildly embarrassing, but now I felt totally ashamed. At the same time, I was cognizant of the fact that I had been through a lot and that this was my way of asking for help. I felt China's heart going out to me, as her eyes welled up in response to my emotionality, and her empathic response made me think that she would be the perfect analyst for me—at least for the duration of my stay in Rio. For some reason, I had the idea that she would empower me. I also thought that if she empathized so deeply with my desires, she might end up going to bed with me.

"Dr. Dentata," I managed to stammer through my tears.

"Just call me China," she said, reiterating what she'd said to me the first time we'd met.

"Oh, my experience is that most analysts like to be called Dr. and refer to their patients as Mr. or Ms."

"Yes, but there has been a whole breakdown in the notion of analytic neutrality," China explained. "Basically, the world has been turned upside down. Patients are becoming friends with their analysts, and in some cases even sleeping with them. The idea of the analyst as a distant figure who should be a tabula rasa, a vehicle for transference, has been disproven. It was becoming obvious that patients knew a lot about their analysts, and that to pretend otherwise was patently dishonest. Analysts who once watched their beautiful patients suggestively hike up their skirts in silence have become freer to express themselves. It's like the Russian Revolution. Neutrality and professionalism are now looked on as Czarist, as forces of repression to be toppled. There was some precedent for this during the '60s in the Sullivanian communes in New York, where doctors slept with their patients, exclusivity and possessiveness were frowned on and boundaries broken. But this is the first time we have seen this kind of change in analytic technique on such a mass scale."

"So, can I make an appointment?" I ventured.

"Would you like to come back to my room?" Schmucker fixed his gaze on me when China posed this question, looking at me with a mixture of pity and beneficence, as if he were a priest bestowing forgiveness. At this point I can only say this: careful what you wish for. Here I was getting an invitation to analysis and what looked like a proposition for sex all in one shot. It was every patient's dream come true, but I suppose I shouldn't have been surprised that such serendipity would occur in a city that stood on the edge of the heart of darkness, with its primitive tribal history and huge Amazonian wilderness.

"I just want to make sure I don't miss the lecture on erotomania," China added wistfully.

China looked at me quizzically when I responded: "It would be great if you could fit me in." I wanted to get into the brisk rhythm that I'd imagined for my analysis. In truth I was a bit taken aback by China's willingness to have me come right up to her room. I have always wanted to enter my analysts' inner sancta, but now that I was given access, I was apprehensive. I didn't want to know China's inner workings. I wanted to keep her at a distance as the idealized parent who would one day rescue me from myself. I was concerned that her analytic couch was in fact her bed. If we proceeded to undertake a full analysis, and simultaneously began an affair in keeping with the latest trends in analysis, where would I find the time to meet whores? I still hadn't been to The Gringo.

Schmucker was wearing his customary outfit—blue blazer, rep tie, and thick rubber-soled shoes. I wondered if there was a chain of stores that catered to analysts like Schmucker, supplying certified non-descript attire. I was aware that he seemed to be disturbed about something. He was fidgeting with the check and seemed to be reading over the figures with great concern.

"I think I had more than you," Schmucker said. "I had three eggs over, bacon, juice, and toast, and you only had two scrambled eggs."

"Why don't we split it right down the middle," came China's endearing response.

Even though I make a good amount of money as a CPA, I have always been particularly careful in negotiating my fees with analysts. The fact that China exuded an air of magnanimity when it came to financial matters was encouraging to me. Although I could already have been negatively transferring, I also got the impression that Schmucker was smirking to himself about getting a few slices of bacon at her expense.

Once the bill was settled, I followed China across the lobby. Her clothes looked so good on her that I couldn't stop thinking about taking them off. Clearly, I was already getting my wires crossed. Whenever I picked up a hooker back in the States, I would inevitably follow her to the sleazy hotel she used with her customers. Once again, I was following a sexy woman whom I was about to pay, even if nominally it wasn't for sex. But I knew that even if China wasn't a hooker, there was some relief in store. I would be able to say whatever came to my mind, even if it was something lurid about my analyst, like the fact that she dressed like a little whore and I wanted to reach under her flowery skirt and pull her little thong down to her ankles and then fuck her in the doggy position. I made a firm commitment to myself that I would tell her this and anything else that came into my head, no matter how embarrassed I felt or how difficult it was to utter the words. I'd never had a woman analyst before, so expressing my desires to her would be a first. Had I chosen Schmucker as my analyst, I would have found myself in the position of criticizing him for being a weak asexual male. I would have told him that I felt superior to him because I would be the winner in the imagined contest I was having with him for China's affections. The triumph was so real to me that I was already feeling Oedipal guilt for vanquishing the father figure in the competitive struggle for mommy's love.

China was wearing high sandals that laced up around her calves and a tight-fitting leotard top that accentuated her pert breasts, whose nipples were already hardened by the time we stood facing each other in the elevator. Besides her Japanese background, China plainly had some Chinese blood in her too. In fact, she looked a little like Chiang Kai-shek. I wondered if she was of aristocratic lineage. Perhaps she was Chiang's great granddaughter. Maybe her great grandparents had even witnessed the Long March, in which Mao and his Communist forces retreated from the Kuomintang. Perhaps they'd even known Sun Yat-sen, the founder of the Chinese Republic. I suddenly had an urge to ask her about the status of Taiwan and the two small islands of Kimoy and Matsu. To mitigate my nervousness, I attempted some banal small talk. "I've never actually walked into an appointment accompanied by my analyst," I said. "Usually my analyst is already there."

"Yes, usually the analyst is seeing other patients before and after your appointment," China replied somewhat blandly. "It's different now because I am not waiting for you, and you probably don't anticipate taking leave of me in the normal manner after your session has ended. This breakdown in the normal order of things is causing an upsurge of fantasies that you may not be entirely ready to handle. There may be fantasies of triumph, and countervailing fantasies of retribution for the success you are afraid you don't deserve."

The elevator swooped up to the twelfth floor and I followed China out. I started to shake as we walked down the long corridor. I began to worry that I was going to pee in my pants, even though I still wasn't wearing any. China swiped her key card and ushered me into her suite. When I saw how neat and clean everything was, I decided that the air of order and calm must have been an indication of her Taoist origins.

Her room had a beautiful view of the ocean. I immediately started to compare it to mine, which only had the so-called "garden view," meaning that it looked out on the enormous condensers that cooled my wing of the hotel. I was feeling short-changed, which, of course, was only more grist for the analytic mill. Some women experience classical penis envy, but I had always suffered from vagina envy. I wanted to be a beautiful woman who was taken care of by rich men, and who effortlessly commanded the kind of view that I was looking at now. I was tired of being a guy who had to scrape his way through life, depending on the kindness of concierges. Our rooms epitomized the two different worlds that we operated in. My room had practically no natural light, while hers was filled with a blinding sunlight that I imagined illuminated every fold of the organ that rhymed with her name. I was fortunate to have an analyst whose name evoked the very organ I so envied. I knew that sex-change operations were possible, but in the end I am not an adventurous spirit. If I got a vagina, I would be limited to having lesbian relationships with Tiffanys. I wasn't sure how I was going to resolve these feelings. I both wanted to be a woman and to fuck them.

China pulled the chair out from her writing desk, which was equipped with a phone and fax machine. She nonchalantly flipped her television to CNN and proceeded to slide into her armchair, affording her a good view of the impressive plasma screen behind my head. The arrangement felt a little odd, but I wanted to let my first one-minute session take its course.

"Well, we'll continue next time," she said without any prompting from me. I got up and immediately sat down again. I knew that China was a Lacanian, but it was as if she were reading my mind. How had she figured out my preferred therapeutic parameters? Each of our initial sessions lasted exactly one minute, and after 16 of them, back-to-back, she went over to her computer and printed out an invoice.

I'd had therapists who made valiant but not always successful attempts to keep their eyes open during sessions. But this was the first time I had an analyst who insisted on watching television while I went on about my problems. What was particularly unfair about it was that, with the television behind me, I couldn't see anything except China's face. This was an unusual configuration for analysis, in which patients and their doctors don't ordinarily make eye contact. In the past, when I'd been in a session with a sleepy therapist, I'd grit my teeth and force myself to talk about the discomfort I was feeling. (In one unfortunate instance, I fell asleep on the couch myself, only to wake up to find that we were both sleeping through the session, my analyst snoring softly behind me.) But I was having trepidation about opening up to China, considering the secret longings I harbored for her.

During most of our early sessions, China watched CNN International, but there were times when I could see she was bored or irritated by the news, especially reports about the refusal of the Chinese to revalue their currency. At these moments, she picked up the remote and switched to a sports network that carried soccer games. She loved the Brazilian team, but she also turned out to be a major David Beckham fan, and felt the best thing that ever happened to the American economy was recruiting Beckham for the Los Angeles Galaxy. On several occasions, I tried to talk about my personal history and early upbringing, but it was hard to get a word in edgewise, between China's vexation about currency fluctuations and her lusty enthusiasm for *futebol.*

"You know what they did to the Iraqi soccer team when they lost under Saddam Hussein? They tortured them." I wasn't sure if China was recommending torture over steroids, but I began to suspect that there might be a method to her madness, and that all her television watching was some new Lacanian technique aimed at causing my long-repressed emotions to spew forth. I got the distinct feeling that she discounted the importance of my early years and my long-winded recollections of playing with those pink Spalding rubber balls in Kew Gardens. I wasn't sure which parts of my past were of analytic significance, and with only a minute per session, it was often difficult to discriminate.

Only 32 minutes had passed, but I had already paid my bill for two months worth of sessions and I could feel a sea change in my personality. China had excused herself to go to the bathroom, and through the door I could hear her tinkling. In all my years of therapy, I had never seen or heard a shrink go to the bathroom, and there were times when I had the distinct feeling that, like parthenogenesis, in which fertilization occurs without the necessity of insemination, there were therapists who never went to the bathroom at all. China was plainly someone who pissed and shat as we all do. She was a real person.

At first I thought it was my imagination, but I started to notice that there were moments when China was actually paying more attention to me than to the television, and I wondered if her kindly gaze was showing far more than mere compassion for the sufferings of her patient. I wasn't sure exactly what to do, but I realized that this was a situation in which all my years of paying for sex would come in handy—if only I could endure 16 more minutes before asking her if I could purchase some kind of sexual service along with the psychoanalysis. (It would be rude to interrupt in the middle of a billing cycle.)

There are many men and women for whom sex isn't a financial transaction. After all, not all women are whores, even in a place like Rio. But a situation in which I was already paying for a woman's services as a therapist segued naturally, in my mind at least, into offering her compensation to slake my carnal desires.

Despite the question of whether our analysis would evolve into prostitution, and the puzzle as to why China insisted on keeping the television on during our sessions, this early period of the analysis, especially the first 192 sessions (the equivalent of a year's worth in a little over three hours), were some of the most fulfilling of all the work we would do together. In fact, we were so engrossed in the analysis that we both forgot about the erotomania lecture we were supposed to attend. About halfway through that first "year," I discovered that China was not wearing underpants, and from what I could see, China's vagina was a hairy one. The effect of her all-natural bush was rather dramatic in exciting the drives that were the essence of my manhood. It took me a while to get up the courage to talk to China about the fact that I could see her vagina and that it was having an effect on the analysis, but when I did she was remarkably calm in response, saying only, "I was wondering how long you were going to continue denying what was right in front of your eyes."

Naturally, this also brought up childhood memories of my mother, whose vagina was visible to me through the diaphanous nightgowns she insisted on wearing around the house. But China crossed her legs and said, "We'll continue next time," just as I was about to address the memories that the constant exposure to my mother's genitals elicited in me.

Even though the next session would start seconds later, it was always a major break in momentum for me. I found myself behaving as if I were a patient in any conventional therapy, first talking about how I was feeling that day before reviewing the themes I had brought up in previous sessions, if I could remember them. For years, my therapists and analysts had told me that the tendency to forget or repress is totally natural, but I found it upsetting that the frequent interruptions totally disrupted my chain of thought.

Of course, I could have proposed that we abandon the Lacanian approach and undertake a shorter number of sessions of the traditional 50-minute length, but I wanted to return from my vacation able to tell everyone I knew that I'd not only had sex with a lot of beautiful Brazilian Tiffanys, but that I'd undergone a complete analysis to boot.

At one point, China asked me if she reminded me of my

mother. My first response was, "Why do you ask?" Analysts never answer when you pose a question, and never respond when you pour out your heart. In any case, the session was over before we could delve any further into the subject, and by the time we started our next session, I had forgotten why I'd even asked the question.

It struck me as obvious that she should ask me if she reminded me of my mother—after all, she was a woman and she was exhibiting her cunt to me just the way my mother had. If anyone was guilty of not being forthcoming, it was I. I was the one who was resistant to seeing the connection. I was the one who was avoiding analytic insight by posing the kind of rhetorical question a logical positivist might ask, rather than allowing my mind to soar to a vibrant state of free association. I was the one who was being literal, who didn't understand the symbolic, metaphoric element that existed in all things. Of course, China didn't look like my mother. She was much better looking.

Even in Lacanian analyses there are relatively long periods of time when nothing seems to happen. In my case, ten minutes passing could seem like a lifetime, since over ten sessions were involved. In actuality, the subject of the relationship between China and my mother's vagina would eventually become more prominent and take up even more time than that. Psychoanalysis is often invidiously compared to short-term behavioral therapy or drug regimens, in which a good degree of affect modulation can become apparent in fewer than ten visits. My analysis with China was paradoxical, in that while it was nominally long-term analysis, it was taking place in much less time than your classic short-term therapy would. But, living in a universe in which the uncertainty principle was used to explain the facts of life, I was not at all surprised by the existence of such contradictions. All these ideas were swimming in my head, but I rarely had a chance to communicate them to China, who seemed constantly prepared to end a session the moment it began. There was no doubt that her insistence on keeping to the therapeutic regimen we had established was an attempt to make a point about the limits of what an analytic session could be.

I looked at this relatively long middle stretch of the analysis, which in the end must have added up to a full day's work, as the period in which we forged a true therapeutic bond. I was learning to trust China even at those moments when she pulled her legs into her chest so that I was looking straight up her snatch. This is what is known in analysis as "working through." I was coming to terms with the distrust I felt toward my mother during my childhood, a period of my life when I was powerless to do anything about the stimulation I experienced.

What was emerging from the therapeutic interaction was the notion that, under normal circumstances, if I met a woman like China who showed me her vagina, I was totally empowered to touch it. I could even enjoy the notion that I might like to stick my penis into it. I think we agreed that in a situation like this, it was imperative that I follow the laws of whatever land I was in, being careful to ask permission prior to insertion.

In retrospect, I think that seeing China's vagina for so many sessions in a row, particularly in the early period of the analysis, had a profound effect on our relationship. Analysis has come a long way from the days when the analyst was regarded as a distant figure who rarely uttered a word. Many of the blatantly non-egalitarian elements of the relationship (in particular, the one in which the therapist gets to know everything about the patient, but the patient knows virtually nothing about the person treating him) have been legislated out of existence in some of the recent amendments to the Civil Rights Act of 1968. The study of transference can no longer be used as a vehicle for discriminatory behavior against patients. I am thankful to the great civil rights leaders of the '60s, like Dr. Martin Luther King, Jr., who in bringing about racial equality also opened the doors for affluent analytic patients whose rights were being violated on the Upper East Side by double standards that evoked the plantations of the Old South. Patients in analysis were no longer treated like indentured slaves who toiled to pay for their therapy and often received little in return. On the other hand, what was going on between China and me was perhaps going a step beyond the liberties that had been envisioned by the courageous freedom fighters who had come before us.

After our 480th session came to a close at the end of the first day, I decided to go out on the town to see what kind of effect my newly gleaned insights had on my relationships with the local Tiffanys. I had to get out of the frying pan and into the fire, as it were, and The Gringo was probably the best place to start.

The acquisition of knowledge can be a double-edged sword. As I walked through the lobby of the hotel, I found that my view of the world had changed. I was painfully aware that looking for Tiffanys had become a job, and that my mind, and heart, was hopelessly preoccupied with China.

I had been a good student at Columbia and always got my assignments in on time. If my reason for coming to Rio was to fuck as many prostitutes as possible, I was going to do my homework and turn in the term paper, or in this case give the oral report. But my heart wasn't in it. My face wasn't hot and I didn't experience skin respiration when I thought of Tiffanys.

I was like a ghost walking through the lobby. I didn't even stop at the concierge desk to speak to Adolphe. Soon enough, I was filled with still more trepidation. There are many rough barrios in Rio, and I'd heard that there were some occasions when sex tourists were susceptible to being mugged—for example, when they got stinking drunk in the Copa and someone slipped them a Mickey and rolled them. More commonly, their minds were so consumed with desire they were unaware of dangerous characters who leaped out of doorways with machetes and lopped off their protruding sex organs. The more passionate they were, the more likely they were to be relieved of their money-clip or even their penis by a Tiffany who also happened to be a serial castrator, a Jack the Ripper in reverse. I didn't want to get sidetracked, let alone victimized, by extraneous carnal desires. I had to stay focused on one question: could I allow myself to seriously contemplate the notion of having an affair, let alone a full-blown relationship, with my analyst? I was reminded of the predicament faced by the Duke of Windsor, who abdicated the throne to marry the woman he loved. Of course, I didn't have to abdicate anything, but I sensed in myself the willingness to go to similar lengths. Perhaps what I was thinking about was abdicating my role as patient in order to become China's lover for the remainder of my vacation in Rio.

I found myself watching the sunset from the Copa, wondering if China played with herself after a long day of seeing patients. I could only imagine what a woman who thought nothing of exposing herself to her patients would do when left to her own devices. I suddenly felt jealous of her fingers for being able to climb their way into the orifices I longed to fondle. Seeing that she was part of the army of therapists who devote their lives to fighting the repression of human instinct, I could only wonder about the extent of the liberties she took with her own body. I imagined her throwing off her little skirt, turning up the volume on her television, and wildly finger-fucking herself while she watched the Brazilian team slam home another penalty kick. She reminded me of Pussy Galore and Lotta Vagina and the rest of the great cinematic heroines named for their phenomenal private parts. I stared out at the sea, whose surface was as calm as glass, noticing a few stray Tiffanys emerging from the surf in their string bikinis. The lazy Rio afternoon would give way to a torrid night of sex for hire, and all I could think about was bursting into China's room to demand emergency therapy.

I would tell her that I loved her and would be willing to pay twice her usual rate if she would only consent to breaking down the barrier of therapeutic discretion and turning our suggestive talk into action. I felt that she held a power and knowledge that would be unleashed in me if only I could stick my penis into her. It was like siphoning fuel from a car.

I was so lost in my thoughts that I was caught off guard when an elegantly attired gentleman, who, with his thin moustache, bore an uncanny resemblance to Salvador Dali, came up to me and asked if I was staying at the hotel. After I informed him that I was indeed a guest, adding that I had obtained observer status at the analytic conference and had even begun my own analysis, he discretely pointed out that I might want to consider slipping into a pair of trousers. I explained to him that I would return to my room as soon as I recovered from the separation anxiety I was feeling from having to part with China for the night. The gentleman, not conversant in the language of psychoanalysis, probably thought I was upset at being separated from a set of expensive dishes. When he looked at me like I was crazy, I reassured him by saying, "That's just an American joke. My pants are being pressed. I'm sure house services must have returned them to my room by now."

I did an about-face and headed to the elevator bank. I figured I might as well go back to my room, but I was suddenly troubled by the thought that my analysis was preventing both China and me from attending the conference. This was as good a reason as any to knock on the door of her room, especially since we had both just missed the lecture on erotomania.

I firmly expected China to be surprised, if not annoyed, to find me standing at her door. But I had rationalized my behavior in such a way that I felt perfectly comfortable telling her that it was a life-or-death matter, even though it was obvious to anyone that missing a lecture was no justification for arriving pant-less and unannounced at your analyst's office-cum-hotel room.

In my overwrought state, I became distracted by one of the many Tiffanys who roamed freely in the hotel corridors. Her microskirt and lizard-skin platform high heels gave me a momentary case of vertigo, so when I knocked on the door of room 1169, I was sure it was room 1269. After knocking once with no answer, I tried again with a little more insistence. Finally I heard footsteps, and before I knew it a Tiffany, buck-naked except for her high heels, appeared at the door and asked nonchalantly in heavily accented English, "Are you here for the orgy?"

In the background, I could see a Tiffany who reminded me of Eurydice in *Black Orpheus*, sitting on the face of an older man. Even though I couldn't see much of him, I made a quick guess that he was an American Midwesterner. He looked like a beached whale, with his hairy stomach flopping off to one side as he lay on his back.

For a moment I thought that I might have interrupted one of China's group sessions. Most analysts don't conduct group therapy, but China wasn't exactly orthodox. Any analyst who shows her vagina to a patient doesn't fall into the classic mode. I asked if anyone had seen China. The black Eurydice must have thought I said "vagina" since she replied, "There's plenty of that here, honey. Why don't you just go into the green room and take off your clothes?"

It was only after I entered the suite that I noticed the video equipment and realized that I had walked onto the set of an S&M film, in this case a remake of Lubitsch's *The Blue Angel*, replete with a masochistic professor and nightclub vamps. The professor was being played by the guy with the hairy stomach. In this version, the Marlene Dietrich character sat on his face. I had never aspired to be an actor, and while I was attracted to the bevy of young Tiffanys, I didn't entertain the possibility that I could successfully audition for a role. In addition, my *reality* was beginning to burn a hole in my pocket. After all my abortive attempts at consummation, I needed to pay someone for sex or therapy, or both. The lure of any fame or fortune I might have inadvertently experienced as a porn star paled in comparison with the pleasure I derived from paying for sex.

With a sigh of regret I closed the Pandora's box of untold perversions and headed one flight up to seek my China. I was under the illusion that I was on an important mission that would affect the nature of what analysts call the compromise formation, which develops as a patient comes to terms with his inner conflicts. In one sense, I was cutting off my nose to spite my face, since by informing her of the fact that we were missing the convention, I was potentially curtailing the amount of time she would have to spend with me.

I walked down the hallway of the twelfth floor with trepidation. I had heard rumors among the analysts at the conference that China's grandmother was one of the first Chinese psychoanalysts in Peking, and that her career was cut short by Mao's Cultural Revolution. Being a strong woman, China's grandmother would not be stopped by the infamous Band of Four, and the type of Lacanian analysis that China herself practiced had its roots, the rumor went, in her mother's need to conclude her sessions abruptly when Communist cadres appeared at her door and forced her to get back to rooting potatoes.

My knees were shaking as I knocked on China's door. Undoubtedly, she would interpret my appearance as having a significance that went deeper than a mere scheduling conflict. That is one of the problems with analysis—nothing is ever accepted as having a mundane meaning. I knocked very softly, somehow thinking that China was sitting on tenterhooks awaiting my arrival. (My tendency to believe that the world revolves around me is one of the subjects we had discussed in a memorable one-minute session.) When there was no answer, I realized that I was being unrealistic. I decided that if I was going to knock on her door, I had to really knock. With the edge of my fist I pounded once more. The doors in the hotel were quite thick, in all likelihood purpose-built to muffle the constant ululations of the guests. But when I put my ear right up against China's door, I could hear the murmurings of CNN. For a moment, I thought that she might very well be seeing another patient. Of course, she could also have simply been relaxing and watching television, though I had a sneaking suspicion that China was a workaholic who only allowed herself to watch TV when she was doing something else. Like many analysts I had encountered, she undoubtedly was very committed to her work—writing papers, attending conferences and teaching, in addition to seeing patients.

As I was about to give up and walk away, thinking that she simply couldn't hear me over the din of the television, a repressed memory was liberated in me and I recalled that the last time I had been in analysis, I'd rung a buzzer that was located conveniently halfway down the door jamb, near the knob of the door which led into my former doctor's office. I took a deep breath, searched for a bell and, finding it, rang. I don't know what I expected. Did I expect China to come wafting across the floor of her suite, flashing her vagina at me as she opened the door? Would I discover an expectant China? Patients always fantasize about what their analysts do in their spare time. In my case, I imagined that China and her beloved Schmucker had ordered up a gourmet meal and that they were dining by candlelight as the full moon cast a magical light over the sand and sea beyond the Copacabana.

When I was a little boy, I would climb into my parents' bed in the middle of the night when I was awakened by a bad dream. Now I wanted to crawl into China's bed—not because I was having a bad dream, but because I wanted to fuck her. Even I was surprised by the intensity of these forbidden thoughts. It's one thing to read about the Oedipus complex in a textbook, but quite another to see it in action. When such transgressive desires stare you in the face, they can cause the kind of guilt that now flooded my brain.

I rang the bell again and again. If I was already on my way to hell, I might as well fly off in a hand basket. If China wasn't there, I would raise her up from the underworld with an unholy racket and exorcise my demons at the same time. I became convinced that even though she wasn't in the room, she could still hear the buzzer, wherever she was. I must have been ringing on and off for a good half-hour before China came to the door, wearing a black lacey bra, high heels, and nothing else.

Analysts insist on seeing their patients four and sometimes five days a week because each session opens up the doors of the unconscious, and in order to allow upsetting emotions to emerge on any given day, a patient needs the reassurance of knowing there will be another session the following day. I was plainly running to China because I needed to follow up on some anxiety that'd been evoked in our last session, i.e., my increasing attraction to her, which I'd subverted with some superficial nonsense about missing the conference. Seeing China for the first time without her clothes on, I was faced with a totally new problem. Hopefully this encounter with her naked body was something that I could deal with the next day in analysis. Barring that, she might be willing to work through things right then and there.

Staring at China, my vision momentarily clouded over. I could see her face, but after the initial shock of seeing her nakedness, I could only see a dark blur when my eyes traveled down to her glorious bush. All of a sudden I found myself in her arms. I was not able to recollect the activity that ensued, but I was sure it would come back to me later as déjà vu, especially if we had finally ended up having sex. At the very least, I imagined that it was better than any foreplay that Johnny Holmes, the legendary Buttman, or any of the great porn stars had ever enacted.

The downside was that it had occurred without a concomitant facility to appreciate it, or even to know it was happening. It reminded me of the old philosophical question: if a tree falls in the forest and no one is there to hear it, does it make a sound?

I had my wits about me enough to know that whatever was happening would be a subject of discussion in our next analytic session. What goes on between analyst and patient is the substance of analysis itself; it is the content of the transference, significant in that it shows the patient the behaviors and emotions he demonstrates in all situations of his life. I was having fantasies about my analyst similar to the ones I had with all the women in my life—except of course my mother. I imagined fucking them, which wasn't surprising since the women I was attracted to were inevitably prostitutes, whose role in life is to entice men into paying them for sex.

The hotel room was now cast in shadows. We lay in each other's arms and then switched into the spoon position, which is how we slept for the next forty-five minutes, a span of time that exceeded any of our sessions. Yes, I was in room 1269, but the space was totally transformed—not only was it dark, but there was no television on. When I awakened, I was sure that this was going to be it. My penis was swollen and looked like one of those booster rockets that sends the space shuttle into the stratosphere, but my expectations for consummation and release were disappointed when China jumped out of bed and cried out, "I'm missing Germany and Spain!" I'd fallen into a deep sleep and was disorientated for a moment. Could our passionate prelude have created sudden longings of the Teutonic and Castilian varieties? I wondered why she had chosen the European Union when she was of Japanese and Chinese descent. But then I realized that as an avid soccer fan, she was talking about the championship match that was occurring that day. She flipped on the lights so she could find the remote, and for the first time I was able to see my analyst from head to toe in all her nakedness. Like the aristocratic Tiffany I met at The Catwalk, she too had a dramatic Venus mound and large dark nipples of the kind I have found prevalent among women of Asian extraction.

My mind was suddenly racing with all the new issues the prospect of a sexual act with my analyst raised—issues that I plainly hadn't wanted to face. Among them was whether I could now call China Tiffany. I was paying China and was at least on the verge of having sex with her. But the payments were for psychoanalysis, and I wasn't sure that the money I forked over for our sessions could be credited toward sex. There was also the question of professional ethics and the fact that China was taking unfair advantage of me due to the strong transference I was experiencing. But if we looked at the counter-transference—the fantasies and feelings the analyst has about his or her patient—the tables could be turned and I could be accused of taking advantage of her. In the end, the financial issue was shaping up to be the biggest mountain I would have to climb, and I was beginning to realize that I might have to pay my analyst separately for sex if I was going to continue having an amorous relationship with her while in treatment.

Despite the fact that I knew I would probably have to wait until the next day's sessions to address the question of actual lovemaking, I expected China would have plenty to say. After all, while there have been cases of analysts sleeping with their patients, it's not exactly business as usual. It can also be cause for an analyst to lose his or her professional accreditation. Naturally, I wasn't going to turn China in, but I thought she would at least exhibit some misgivings about her behavior, or show some sign that what had transpired was out of the ordinary. At the very least she would acknowledge that our interaction had a modicum of significance. But as I got out of bed to retrieve my bikini briefs and seersucker jacket, I was hard put to get her attention at all. She was totally riveted by the soccer match. She was perfectly willing to agree with my observations when I commented "good save" or "nice pass," but when I tried to inject a personal note by referring to the fact that we had a session the next day, she shushed me. I couldn't take my eyes off China's vagina, but I knew I had to leave if I was ever going to get to The Gringo. No matter how badly I wanted to fuck China, I made a commitment to myself to go back to my hotel room and put on a pair of slacks. I realized that China was an analyst at heart and could never be a real prostitute, no matter how hard she tried. Even if I could pay her for sex, she would never qualify as a real whore in Rio or anywhere else.

I tried to tell myself that I was just a normal male who wanted to get laid. In a place like Rio, if you believe the travel literature, it's easier to do than breathing on a smoggy day. My denial notwithstanding, I knew that a sea change was going on inside of me and that the last shreds of my rationality were quite possibly slipping away. I immediately ran back to my hotel room to change into the extra pair of seersucker slacks that my mother always taught me to bring on trips in case I stained myself. But they no longer looked right. Instead, I had an urge to wear tight jeans that outlined my crotch. My failure to get my rocks off in one of the world's great sex capitals, at least while conscious, was changing me. Even though The Gringo was loaded with Tiffanys who preferred men whose pockets were stuffed with *reality*, I still wanted to show off my other assets. I was tired of dressing up like a nice Jewish accountant, feigning respectability in my Brooks Brothers attire.

I was suddenly filled with a sense of mortality. Confronted with the specter of my inevitable demise, I wanted to live life to the hilt, to be as sexy as the Tiffanys whose services I sought. I wanted prostitutes to stare at my crotch just as eagerly as I stared at theirs.

I could easily have walked out into the local marketplace and found a shop that sold tight jeans, but I felt an inexplicable rush of prudish misgivings about walking around the lobby of the hotel in my bikini underwear. I called down to the concierge's desk and explained my problem to the woman who answered. She told me she would have to come up to measure me so she could procure the jeans I needed.

When she came up to the room, the first thing I noticed was the gold nametag that was pinned to her breast. It read

"Tiffany." Dropping all pretenses, she hiked up her skirt so I could see what she had underneath. The only problem was that she shaved. Even though I had come to Brazil for sex, I dreaded Brazilian hot waxing, which I still couldn't help but associate with pedophilia.

"I guess you're not a Tiffany in name only," I managed to say. Her skirt still rolled up to her waist, Tiffany sauntered over to my room's entertainment console and switched to a channel featuring '70s disco tunes.

"In Brazil, prostitution is totally legal and in fact encouraged, since sex tourism is such a vital part of our economy," Tiffany volunteered as she danced with her skirt hiked up and her hands held behind her head. "I learned English in school so that I could communicate with the customers I started to see as soon as I turned 18 and my parents felt I was ready to turn tricks."

"It's great that your parents encouraged your independence."

"I learned that my body was a commodity. People often think of Brazil as a third-world country, but we have an exceptional educational system. I learned about Joseph Schumpeter's concept of creative destruction in high school history. It's what finally made me see how I could effectively exploit my own assets." Many American women remain too attached to their parents to become whores, so I found Tiffany's liberal upbringing and her references to the famed Schumpeter work, *Capitalism, Socialism and Democracy*, to which most American secondary school teachers only give a polite nod, to be enlightening. After primping herself in the bathroom, Tiffany returned to the initial reason for her visit and began to measure my crotch for the tight jeans she was going to procure. She pulled my penis out, measured it, and said "six" with a knowing smile.

"But I'm not six inches," I said, looking at the shriveled carrot that was left in the wake of my unconsummated foreplay with China.

"Fully extended it's an easy six," she said. She even measured my balls and wrote down a two on her pad, indicating, I suppose, that they were both accounted for.

The speed with which my jeans arrived made me wonder if this wasn't some kind of racket. I imagined a sweatshop in the basement of the hotel filled with illegal immigrants toiling day and night to fit the made-to-order desires of American guys who wanted to accentuate their penis size. In America I might not have wanted to broadcast the fact that I had a substantial package, since many of the girls who work the streets will do anything to avoid the kind of stud who is going to leave them hobbling in their platform shoes.

One of the toothless Brazilian cleaning women brought up the pants. No sooner was I holding them against my waist to check the length than Tiffany had hooked her fingers over the bottom edge of her tiny skirt and was threatening to pull it up. I closed my eyes and begged her not to tempt me again, as it would ruin my meal. I'm referring of course to the constant warning I used to get from my parents about not eating too many hot buns when we went out for dinner, lest they spoil my appetite. I have a different attitude about buns now that I'm a grown man—I believe that if you want to gorge yourself on buns, you should go right ahead. True, I had come to Brazil to have a good time with as many girls as possible. But as charming and professional as Tiffany was, I really had to start playing the field. It's like people who go to France to see the sites. The Eiffel Tower is nice, but you also want to go to Chartres, Mont St. Michel, the Louvre, Versailles, Aix en Provence, and naturally, Pigalle, which is still filled with clubs populated by decrepit, overpriced hookers

If it's not your habitual attire, pulling on a pair of tight jeans can be a problem. I'd already had one go-around with jeans on this trip, but the pair Tiffany had ordered for me were no comparison. They were more like a leotard than Levi's, and just getting the legs on took every ounce of strength I had. I had no idea how I was going to actually pull them up over my thighs, buttocks and, most importantly, my crotch. Because I am someone with an extreme aversion to physical pain, mixed with a rather acute case of castration anxiety, I toyed with the notion of actually wearing the jeans around my thighs like someone who had just gotten up from the toilet and has forgotten to pull his pants up. Once, when I was hunting Tiffanys in Tijuana, I actually saw a group of vacationers who had been suffering from Montezuma's revenge for days and had stopped bothering to pull up their pants at all. But I realized that I wasn't going to accomplish my purpose if I didn't bite the bullet and try to get the pants up as best I could.

There is an old expression that is popular in the recovery movement—One Day at a Time. I decided to apply this philosophy to my jeans, which I began to pull up one centimeter at a time, even though I was afraid my circulation could be cut off, possibly resulting in the loss of a testicle.

Most Latin American men are adept at situating their testicles in tight pants to optimize their crotch appeal. It's a mating custom that has evolutionary roots, and as vivid an illustration of Darwinian natural selection as a peacock's feathers. But while it is a distinctly biological matter, it is something that is reinforced through education. Brazilian boys are taught how to climb into extremely tight jeans when their penises and testicles are still small. Gradually, as they develop, they are able to accommodate an ever-larger package, making concessions to morphology by buying larger sizes without compromising their crotch display.

In North American society, where brainpower plays a larger role in the survival and propagation of the species, far less importance is accorded to exhibiting the male genitalia. American boys attend SAT prep classes while their Latin American counterparts are learning to display their penises. So while I was busy cramming for my college entrance exams, my Brazilian and

Latin American peers were busy cramming their packages into skin-tight dungarees.

Tiffany was certainly deserving of some kind of award for concierges who go beyond the call of duty to make sure their guests have a comfortable stay. She earned my vote when she pulled her skirt up to her waist so that she could kneel down to massage and lick my balls while easing them into the snug confines of my jeans. In the process, I got another view of her vagina, which unfortunately made me even more homesick for China than I already was. And while she was trying to be of help, she ended up exacerbating the problem by giving me a hard-on.

Fortunately, man is an adaptable creature, and even a North American male who is reliant on brainpower to attract the opposite sex is able to adopt the customs of a totally different culture. I don't know how I would fare if I had my tongue stretched—part of the mating rituals of some Amazonian tribes—or how I would have accommodated having my feet bound like a Chinese girl living during the dynastic era. But I was certainly able to adjust to having my dick crowded into what seemed at first glance to be an uncomfortably restricted area. I simply equated it to the New Yorker forced to cram all his or her worldly possessions into a tiny studio apartment.

I grew up in the fifties, during the polio epidemic, and when Tiffany and I managed to finally get the jeans on and I took my first steps, I was reminded of the newsreels of little kids hobbled by polio. Unfortunately, I still had an erection, which was impeding my progress. My usual technique for getting rid of erections in addition to thinking about concentration camps, centered on the bombings of Hiroshima and Nagasaki. When that didn't work, I'd think of earthquakes or floods or even serial killers. Conjuring up Richard Nixon's face was always a sure bet if I wanted to lose an erection, and then there was his Secretary of Defense, Melvin Laird, a lock for eliminating erotic thoughts. More contemporary examples, like Donald Rumsfeld, didn't work. The rage was too palpable and only strengthened my woody.

Tiffany was turning out to be the mother I never had—someone who encouraged my sexuality and dressed me in a way that made me attractive to other women. She packed my genitals into the jeans the way an attentive mother would pack her son's lunch box. If I was going to have a lasting relationship with a prostitute, I could do worse than this exceptionally maternal, sexually motivated Tiffany.

When she finally managed to get my fly zipped and my jeans buttoned, Tiffany pushed me away from her and said, smiling broadly, "Let me look at you." I was still wearing my Brooks Brothers seersucker jacket, my bowtie, and my classic button-down collar shirt, along with my Weejuns. I was starting to feel a bit like a fashionista. The mixture of styles was a style in itself, and I think that both Tiffany and I knew that I was going to make quite an impression when I entered The Gringo. Though I assumed that clothes were coming off in the club more than they were being put on, according to Adolphe The Gringo was a fashion Mecca, and it wasn't surprising for prostitutes and their johns to make sartorial statements that impacted the larger populace, where whores and their customers accounted for such a large demographic.

Tiffany offered to blow me one last time, as a freebee, but I politely declined since I wanted to save up my load so I had something to offer when I made my big entrance at the club. I had a momentary desire to go back to room 1269 and show China my new outfit, but I was afraid that, in spite of all that had transpired between us, she might revert to analytic neutrality. For a moment I even thought I was going crazy and that nothing had in fact happened between China and me, that my desires had become so real that I'd crossed the line between fantasy and reality. This is why it's dangerous to have an analyst of the opposite sex. While a normal relationship between two men generally entails an ample homoerotic subtext, adding a romantic dimension to the relationship between a heterosexual male and a female analyst who refuses to wear underpants can engender problems not only with neutrality, but also with the transference, which becomes contaminated.

I started out of the room, but I was forced to move slowly because my pants were chafing the inside of my thighs. Every time I passed women in the hallway they thought I was interested, and since most of them were Tiffanys, they propositioned me. In the short time it took me to get down to the main lobby and then to the ballroom where the sign for the erotomania lecture still stood on its easel, I had been flashed and groped numerous times by the bands of prostitutes who cruised the halls of the hotel. My penis was sore from being engorged and cramped in such a small space. I went over to the placard describing the lecture and lingered over it for a few moments. Erotomania was described on one of the photocopied leaflets piled next to the placard as a pathology that afflicted mostly females who suffered from delusions of being desired, and I found it somewhat anomalous in Rio, where everyone seemed to desire everyone else, with little delusion involved as far as I could see.

I opened up the doors to the ballroom, which was now darkened, its banks of seats totally empty except for a woman's bobbing head. It looked like one of the analysts I had seen at the conference was giving a blowjob to a colleague, and for a moment I experienced a shot of jealousy, thinking it might be China. In any case, the atmosphere in Rio was obviously infectious even for analysts, who generally tend to keep a professional demeanor. I was beginning to understand how Rio could liberate the unconscious desires of practically anyone, including the most intransigent mental health professional. What if it was China giving the blowjob? So what? She was a free agent and so was I. We had no commitments to each other, beyond that of doctor and patient. I had no right to make any demands of her at all. As painful as it all was, China was actually doing me a favor by keeping her distance. My unfulfilled love for her only fueled my lust.

I decided to head out to the Copacabana. It was early evening and I knew that I was at a turning point in the trip. I was no longer waltzing around Rio in my underpants, and in fact had progressed to the point where I was both desirable and plainly eager to make my desires known. Sometimes analytic patients have sessions over the phone, and as I proceeded out onto the Copa, I thought momentarily about calling China in order to air a few lingering anxieties. I just wanted to let China know I was still thinking about our work together, even as I made my way toward the crowds of whores at The Gringo. If I was still thinking about her even as I was dressed to kill and about to get my rocks off, then she must mean something to me. But just as I was about to reach into my jacket pocket for my rented cell phone, it occurred to me that if she was indeed the woman I had spotted in the darkened ballroom, she obviously wouldn't be able to talk. So I returned the phone to my pocket.

Being a New Yorker, I always jaywalk. But with the tight pants I had trouble estimating the time it would take me to get from one side of the street to the other, and a taxicab swerved dramatically to avoid hitting me, nearly sideswiping another car. The driver pulled over, plainly annoyed and cursing loudly, but I couldn't understand the Portuguese. When I screamed back, "Could you express your feelings in English? I'm an American," he simply slammed his car door, gunned his engine, and sped off.

At that moment, standing in the island between two streams of traffic, I was reminded of the fragility of life. I knew that I had to give myself extra time to make it from the traffic island to the other side of the busy avenue. I was hyperventilating, and now that I had finally decided this was the night I would test the depths of human pleasure, I was eager to get to my destination.

I would have run or at least picked up my pace if I could, but I had to wait until there was no traffic in sight to finally cross a street, encumbered as I was by my skin-tight jeans. I had never been bow-legged, but now I noticed I was walking around with my knees pointed outward, like a cowpuncher who spends the day in the saddle rustling up his herd.

Despite being an urban dweller, and more particularly a denizen of Manhattan's Upper West Side, I have become totally dependent on Global Positioning Systems. All the car and cab services use them, and my car is equipped with one. As a result I have lost the ability to follow directions. One of the harbingers of modern life is an attrition of abilities in areas that have been taken over by technology. For instance, even though I'm an accountant by profession, I can barely add or subtract, and have totally lost the ability to multiply and divide. So, as I negotiated the warrens of Tiffany-filled streets that led to The Gringo, I was in a continual state of confusion, not knowing which way I was going. My body was trapped in the contemporary version of a medieval suit of armor, but I was driven on by images of a magnificent world filled with impossibly beautiful prostitutes, like a palace in one of those Disney animations I loved as a kid.

At the very least I can usually rely on my dick as the equivalent of an electronic device leading me toward a scent—specifically the pheromones given off by women whose bodies are for hire—but now I was in a state of total confusion, frequently finding myself turning in circles, growing dizzy and light-headed in the process.

I was actually reminded of the scenes in *Vertigo* when Jimmy Stewart's character experiences the sensations of falling as he relives his traumatic memories. But what was the trauma I was responding to? Was I suffering from a totally experiential problem having to do with the loss of circulation to my genitalia, which could be addressed by an analyst of the so-called existential school, or was my vertigo the result of factors pertaining to depth psychology and the instinctual drives that it addresses? In addition to the constriction of my blood vessels, I was also sweating profusely, and I wanted to find a Tiffany as quickly as possible, if for no other reason than the fact that I needed to get my pants off. It might have been a superficial solution, but I was convinced that as soon as my dick was free to get as hard as it needed to, I would at least be able to retrieve some sense of direction. This is what is known by those seeking spiritual enlightenment as a "limited objective," but I needed to do something before I fainted right in the middle of one of the many boulevards scattered around Rio.

I decided that I would find a fresh Tiffany even before I got to The Gringo and I promised myself to practice some form of *coitus interruptus*, which would whet my appetite for the pleasures that awaited me later in the night.

Memories flashed through my mind as I staved off another fainting spell. There had been an episode in high school, soon after the Beatles became famous, when I'd wanted to be like the other kids and had secretly gone out to buy a pair of tight white Levi's, which fit much like the pants I was wearing now. My penis hadn't grown to its full adult size, so the pants were not nearly as constrictive, and I was easily able to walk around with or without an erection. I was totally embarrassed when my mother discovered them hidden behind a pair of slacks in my closet, but when I asked her if she was mad, she just shrugged and said that she was disappointed in me. I would actually have preferred it if she had gotten angry, because the disconsolate look on her face made it seem as if I had inflicted a mortal wound in my attempt to look sexy and hip.

One of the things that can happen in an intense analysis like the one I was undertaking is that the patient introjects the analyst's persona into his consciousness. So even though there was no China at the present moment, I felt her questioning presence in my mind. Consequently, I began to realize that the trouble I was having with my new pants was partially psychosomatic. The feelings of constriction, I began to understand, were largely in my head. And the faintness came from reliving the trauma of my mother's discovery of my adolescent fashion transgression. It wasn't the pants that were making me feel lightheaded; it was the guilt I felt toward my mother!

Whenever a therapist interviews me for the first time, I make a point of the fact that I've never had any transcendent experiences. I've never seen a great white light. Instead, I endorse a pragmatic spiritualism that is simply a reiteration of the Golden Rule. But now, for the first time, a genuine lightness came over me and I almost felt as if I was levitating. The tightness of the pants no longer seemed to matter. My crotch was no longer locked within the denim that encased it, and I knew I could have as many erections as I wanted regardless of the restricted circumstances in which my penis was operating. I realized at that moment that there are many people who have to make do with extremely meager resources. If whole families with eight or nine children lived in one solitary room, then my cock and balls could certainly survive a cramped walk to The Gringo.

I didn't know if I was hallucinating, but every street sign seemed to be *Revolução* this or *Revolução* that, differentiated only by an appended date. I figured Brazil must have had many revolutions, not the least of which had to do with sex. How did Brazilian society ever get to be such an idyll, a place where women who would have been considered unattainable in other countries freely sold their bodies to a marketplace of men who qualified for their affections only in their willingness to pay? It was truly a wonderful form of commerce, and an example of how free market capitalism can spur the growth of individual initiative.

Suddenly I stopped dead in my tracks, having spotted one of the most beautiful Tiffanys I had ever seen. She was tall and muscular, almost a parody of feminine beauty in the perfection of her features. Her lips were painted bright red and her cleavage was almost bucolic, soothing the eyes with a vision of rolling splendor. I was about to call out to her when I noticed a protruding Adam's apple and realized that the "she" I was about to proposition was really a "he." Besides my earlier encounter with a girl who turned out to be a man, I'd never actually been with a transvestite—though I had heard they could be rather exquisite when you accepted the notion that a vagina wasn't the be-all and end-all.

"Tiffany." I heard the words come out of my mouth breathlessly and involuntarily, as if someone else were actually saying them. She was tall with kinky hair and she seemed to get the idea that I was a foreigner, despite my newly Latinized appearance. "Going out?" she said, in a basso profundo that mocked her otherwise feminine features. I knew the lingo, the shorthand by which hookers communicated their availability to strangers. It was like the universal grammar that Noam Chomsky talks about; it was something that belied the actual words. "Looking for a date?" "Going out?" How many times had I heard the magic words?

Tiffany was light-skinned, a male Naomi Campbell. If there were fashion magazines that used transsexuals as models, I would have recommended that she apply, but I could see how such a career would have been severely compromised by the male genitalia, which would have been difficult to hide in a tight-fitting skirt.

"My name is Ken and I'm an accountant from the Upper West Side of Manhattan. I have a peculiar request and maybe you can help me. You are very beautiful and I would very much like to sleep with you, but I have other plans this evening. However, I would be very happy if you would let me see your breasts so I could take off my pants and liberate my erection. It's a long story, too boring to go into. Just tell me yes with your eyes and I will come forth with the necessary *reality*."

She actually looked like one of the Tahitian women in a Gauguin painting, strong and impassive with a stony expression. She beckoned me to follow her, and as I walked behind her on yet another street named after an uprising, I noticed that she had long, sinewy legs like Kobe Bryant. Still, she walked with a distinctly feminine carriage, moving her hips provocatively, and I had to keep reminding myself that she was a he, and that in all likelihood more surprises lay in store. While I never would have solicited such a creature if I weren't looking to discharge sexual tensions in extraordinary circumstances, I have to confess to a certain curiosity about the strange buffet of organs I was about to see. Trannies are a little like centaurs—some of them have great tits while still being hung like horses.

She stopped in front of a narrow building that looked like a squat or a crack house back in Manhattan. I watched her as she made her way up a narrow, winding staircase that ascended into total darkness. For a moment I asked myself why I was doing this. Was this seemingly reckless behavior just another symptom following on the heels of my recent vertigo? During flu season, a high temperature and fatigue are usually followed by diarrhea. Was my flirtation with danger just another way of acting out against the guilt I felt about wearing forbidden attire?

We ascended two flights in darkness and then Tiffany scampered up to a landing that was lit by a dim bulb hanging from a frayed wire. My curiosity about why she had run so quickly ahead of me despite her high heels was quickly answered when I arrived at the top of the stairs. Tiffany had picked up her skirt and lowered her gaffe, which is the jockstrap-like device that transvestites use to hold their penises between their legs. She had also pulled off her top, and the prominent exemplars of both male and female genitalia made me think I might be dreaming. Tiffany had an exceptionally large penis for someone who wanted to be girl.

I felt a little like Paul Bunyan. Someday that big old penis was going to be chopped down, and I was filled with the irrational fear that I might be the one designated to do it. In my feverish state, my mind was making brilliant but outsized associations. I wanted to get out of there as quickly as possible. "My doctor, whose first name happens to be China, could help you with your vaginal reconstructive surgery," I blurted out.

I noticed that one of Tiffany's hands was behind her back. As she pulled out a knife I realized with terror that it was she who might be playing the part of Paul Bunyan. I'd read about cases of men who had been castrated by angry transvestites. I was hanging out with the wrong person in the wrong place. What was I doing in this squalid atmosphere when I was supposed to be experiencing the exquisite pleasures of The Gringo?

"You see, my friend, this is my trusty shiv," Tiffany growled, dropping all pretense of seduction.

"Oh it's very nice, congratulations," I said nervously. "Shiv, huh, that's such a nice word."

"Yes, it's a term that's very popular among pre-op transsexuals the world over."

"You have a very good vocabulary."

"You mean for someone who is on the lowest rung of the social order?" Tiffany barked back. "I bet you'd be surprised if I told you I have a PhD in anthropology from Stanford."

"Yes, I would. I mean, no, I'm not surprised at all. You seem to have great control of your faculties, and many faculties to control, which would make you a wonderful faculty member anywhere."

Suddenly I remembered the case of a transgender academic at a university in the Midwest who had gone completely crazy right before the final stages of her sex change, just as her penis was to be converted into a vagina. In fact, she had never gone through with her vaginoplasty. Instead, she used a twelve-gauge shotgun to murder her male lover, who had waited years for her to complete the final passage into womanhood. To top it off, she also blew away two army officers who had been recruiting female students to join the Army National Reserve. The whole incident made the front pages of tabloids like *The National Inquirer*, and the murder of the boyfriend was declared a crime of passion, the perpetrator suffering from temporary insanity and receiving consecutive acquittals for the murder of the two recruiters. Still, as I recalled, the murders had caused her to lose her tenure, and what better place for a defrocked pre-op transsexual anthropology professor to find gainful employment than as a hooker on the streets of Rio?

I realized that the shiv was probably not an offer for some new form of S&M sex play involving cutting and piercing. My little adventure in priming the pump might end up initiating a new spree of killings in which I would be the first victim. As if to confirm my worst fears, I suddenly remembered that the killer had gone AWOL from the court-mandated anger management program she had attended in the wake of the attacks.

"Oh China!" I exclaimed, invoking the image of my therapist in a last ditch attempt to regain my composure. China was the wrong word to mention to a transsexual filled with ambivalence about not having either a set of china or a vagina to go along with it, and I stepped backward in horror as she pointed the knife at my throat.

"You're totally immersed in Eurocentric traditions, with their emphasis on gender and the legacy of domination and submission that accompanies the hegemony of the male or female zygote in the matrilineal and patrilineal traditions. Legendary figures like Margaret Mead and Franz Boas created the mythology of modern sexuality, which found its roots in books like Frazier's *The Golden Bough*, a work of great genius, albeit totally wrong-headed, but which showed the growth of the primitive mind to the point where it was able to master figures of speech like synecdoche and metonymy, and thereby enjoy the fruits of an incipient symbolism and even proto-religiosity." I had the feeling Tiffany was just getting warmed up.

"But there are whole other traditions that received little documentation because they run counter to the accepted creeds of chromosomal sexuality, by which XY genes describe a creature defined as being male, with XX being the significant component in directing the formation of so-called female gonads, in particular the ovaries, to which you recently surreptitiously and slyly alluded by crying out the seemingly innocuous "china." I know you think I'm crazy and dangerous and frightening, but you are going to hear me out." In fact, I had no intention of interrupting. Tiffany clearly was in no mood for stichomythic dialogue.

"The fact is that there are cultures and primitive tribes that still exist in the furthest reaches of the Amazonian rain forest, in Sumatra, and to some extent in Borneo, where the dichotomy between males and females has never emerged, and where many so-called men have well-developed mammary glands and have even given birth, in some cases through their anuses. Similarly, there are women with chest hair and large penises, which are really overripe clitorises that hang provocatively from their vaginas. When you tell one of these boys or girls to go fuck themselves, they are literally capable of doing it."

As she finished her rant, she pulled the knife away from my face. I was no longer having any problems with the painful erection in my tight jeans. When I reached down, I was shocked to discover that my penis was nowhere to be found. My prick had made a hasty retreat, squeezing itself up inside of me like a guerilla fighter camouflaging himself in the brush to avoid becoming a target. I checked in my pocket for some *reality*, which I knew I was going to need if I wanted to emerge from this situation in one piece.

For someone like Tiffany, the penis holds no captive value, and I'm sure she would have thought nothing of performing an emergency penectomy if I didn't show proper appreciation for her services. I have come to regard almost everything that happens in human life as a form of therapy, and the present encounter with Tiffany was no exception. Tiffany was helping me work through a deep fear of castration, so when I left her at the top of the stairs, I gave her a nice tip in addition to the tidy sum—$100 worth of *reality*—that was her standard rate. For a transgender PhD anthropologist, Tiffany had a natural entrepreneurial sense of the value of her unique services.

I had gone through a painful process of awareness that was also fraught with a great deal of physical danger, but the evolution of human consciousness always comes at a cost. The paleontologist Stephen J. Gould had shown that fossil records did not show a rational, steady process leading from quadrupeds to bipeds to prehensility and tool making. For a while, I was dating a Tiffany who had acquired post-graduate credits in anthropology at the New School, and besides the boners she gave me, she had also inspired me to bone up on the latest developments in evolution.

I should have been working through my issues with China instead of dallying with a mutant creature whose attributes were better consigned to the x-rated exhibits at the Museum of Sex. I had justified my little deviation as an attempt to deal with one of my psychosexual idiosyncrasies, and also as research into an unfamiliar realm, the ignorance of which I felt was an ellipsis in my sexual education. But it was now clear to me that it was time to return to my primary objective.

I had written the exact address of The Gringo down on a torn piece of hotel stationary—32A Via Revolução Outubro 13. When I came out of the Brazilian equivalent of a SRO that Tiffany had led me to, I was on Via Revolução Março 5. Soon, I spotted another small alley, Via Revolução Abril 15, where a number of beautiful Tiffanys were rhythmically beckoning. I figured this must be the right place to turn, since April was closer to October and, of course, being an accountant, April 15 has mystical associations for me. I could have engaged the services of any of the Tiffanys on Via Revolução Abril 15—one was more beautiful than the next, and as I walked by they all picked up their skirts. After my most recent experience, I began to realize why the whores in Rio were so free about displaying their merchandise. This way there was no doubt about their gender.

As the red light turned to green on the crosswalk of the large thoroughfare marked Boulevard Revolução, the frenzied traffic came to a reluctant stop. I couldn't believe my eyes when, off of another small street in the distance, I saw a huge sign with a pulsating neon arrow and a silhouette of a shapely woman that read "The Café Gringo." I wondered what had happened to the Vias de la Revolução May, June, July, August, and September, but on the whole I was just glad to be there.

But what was I looking for? Did I want to see naked bodies, did I want to achieve orgasm, or was I looking for some sort of love, and hopefully companionship, in my older years? Was I going to The Gringo to find a prostitute I could spend my life with? Was I looking for a true partner, a true relationship? Or was I simply hoping to achieve an explosive, mind-blowing fuck, a fuck of such intensity that it would elevate my consciousness, like an acid trip?

What is pleasure? It's a question I had never addressed during my analysis with China. But I knew there was plenty of time left, by Lacanian standards. If nothing else, I'd learned from China that a lot could be accomplished in a minute, and this observation extended to lovemaking. There is no such thing as premature ejaculation in Lacanian analysis. In fact, what some people call premature ejaculation would be for the average Lacanian analyst a long, intense session of lovemaking.

As I approached The Gringo, I saw Klieg lights and trucks, and could hear the sound of a jackhammer. It reminded me of Manhattan, where Con Ed is always opening up the street to fix steam pipes, although in this case I presumed all the jacking and hammering had to do with intense sexual activity. I'd heard there were all kinds of strange happenings at the club, and that many of the evenings took on the raucous, Dionysian qualities characteristic of radical theater in the '60s, when actors in groups like the Living Theater actually ran naked in the streets, shattering taboos and eventually initiating group sex on a mass scale. In fact, Rio's Carnival, in which thousands of people caroused in the streets for days, had something in common with some of the revolutionary performances I had seen as a student at Columbia, including some memorable experiments in free love. Unfortunately, when I got closer to the club, I saw that all the noise was connected to a far more mundane purpose. It looked like a water main had broken. When I tried to ask what was going on, I encountered the same sphinx-like glare that was popular among Con Ed workers in Manhattan. I went so far as to think that in our cross-cultural era there might even be some sort of exchange program between utility workers from New York and Rio in an attempt to foster mutual understanding. Perhaps I was receiving a bona fide Con Ed brush-off in the middle of Rio.

My heart sunk as I looked through the opened doors of the club to see electrical wires dangling over puddles of water. The lighting system, replete with a classic disco ball, had been disconnected. The only inkling of the club's former splendor was a number of Tiffanys wearing overalls and hardhats who had obviously been hired to help out with the utility work. Their ample bosoms were hanging outside the straps of their overalls, and several were sporting work boots with high heels.

I wasn't sure which way to turn. I could have simply gone back to the Copacabana, but something told me that a whole swath of Rio's sexual life couldn't be short-circuited by a few plumbing and electrical problems. As I prepared to walk back to the Boulevard Revolução, I noticed a short white-haired gentleman in a grubby tee shirt, the stub of a cigar hanging out of the side of his mouth. He looked like the kind of guy who had spent his life as a night watchman and now, in retirement, just watched over things on a recreational basis.

"Do you know if The Gringo moved to temporary quarters?" I bellowed.

He made a sign that he didn't understand what I was talking about, but he also held out a palm to indicate that he would try harder if I gave him money. I placed some *reality* in his palm.

He held his finger to his lips and then said something in Portuguese that I gathered meant that I should follow him. We walked away from the utility trucks and lights and into a warren of side streets, each one seemingly smaller than the last. None of these streets, which were hardly more than cobblestoned footpaths, was large enough to accommodate a car, and I started to notice piles of droppings that I supposed were from horses or donkeys. Rio is an odd series of contrasts; it is an ultra-modern city that at the same time is filled with areas that resonate with the poverty and backwardness of the country's interior. It is a place of hope for rural peasants who come to seek their fortunes. But the ever-present poverty is a reminder of the fact that, for some, the promise of a new life is not that easily attainable.

To be a Tiffany requires a certain degree of sophistication, and many of the women from the small backwaters of the Amazon know little about how to please a man in the way that is necessary to become a real Tiffany. Many of them have never seen a garter belt, black stockings, or a sexy French brassiere. For these peasant women, sex is simply a matter of child bearing. They often have large broods of children who become street urchins and beggars. If only they knew how, these women could be using their bodies to make the kind of big bucks that could get their kids into decent private schools.

Some of the streets were becoming so narrow that the buildings on either side practically touched, so that someone could almost reach out a window to shake the hand of his neighbor across the way. Yes, the hardscrabble existence of the poor had some benefits, not the least of which was a sense of community forged by forced proximity. But I was starting to wonder where my tight-lipped friend was leading me. This didn't look like the kind of area where I was going to find a sex club, although the narrow alleyway reminded me of the crack between a woman's legs. I couldn't help noting that Rio's ubiquitous sexuality was reflected not only in its sleek, shiny hotels and phallic skyscrapers, but also in the architecture of its most impoverished neighborhoods.

As we walked along, I noticed what looked like a hurricane cellar up ahead. My aunt had had one of those at the back of her house on Long Island, and I used to love to sneak down into the basement, which was filled with canned goods and bottled water. She kept these goods in store for the end of the summer season, when storms periodically made their way up the coast, hitting her little town of Long Beach with great fury. I didn't think much of it, nor of the little *Revolução* decal that I noticed affixed to the cellar door as we approached. With all the streets named for one revolution or another, it didn't strike me as unusual to see generic advertisements for revolution on a door. Then I noticed the steady flow of beautiful Tiffanys and tanned Brazilian men in tight, crotch-hugging slacks and open shirts disappearing through the narrow, unlit space into which my friend was now urging me.

I was apprehensive. On the plane I'd read an article about the international slave trade, and while I didn't see myself as a likely candidate for sexual slavery, I was concerned that I might suddenly be drawn into an illegal activity for which I could conceivably be viewed as an accomplice. I have an active imagination, and my free-floating guilt, which was a constant subject of discussion with China, always makes me feel that I am in danger of facing some sort of retribution for imagined crimes. There had been periodic sweeps of Rio's underworld traffic in sex slaves. I had no idea what sights lay before me as I crossed the river Styx into my fantasy Hades.

As it turned out, I was simply wafted along on a wave of uncontrollable lust. As I approached the stairs leading down to the basement of the club, I spotted one of the most beautiful Tiffanys I'd ever seen. She looked like a Cherokee Indian, with straight black hair that hung to the waist of her backless dress. When I got a closer look, she turned out to be even more beautiful than my initial impression—turquoise eyes, pouting lips, and a spectacular ass that made Jennifer Lopez's prodigious fundament look like a ham hock. Following her, I instinctively called out "Tiffany!"

"It's actually Brittany, darling, like the rocky province in France."

"But doesn't that break the Geneva conventions, wherein the UN established Tiffany as the name used for all sex workers?"

She immediately put her finger to her lips and whispered, "Not in Uva. Everyone here is either Brittany or Crystal." It turned out that Uva was a renegade club in many ways, not only because of its Brittanys and Crystals, but also in the unusual practices that were commonplace on the dance floor and in the warren of private back rooms, which were called "Les Caves." As I carefully made my way down the steps into the darkness, using only the glowing flesh of Brittany's ass as a beacon, all I could think of was Britney Spears, another conflicted person who, while she might have made a great Tiffany, was also in need of psychoanalysis.

"You don't look like a Brittany," I said, barely able to control a spontaneous outbreak of tardive dyskinesia, or uncontrollable licking of the lips. I had never wanted a Tiffany as much as I wanted Brittany. I didn't even want my China in the same way, although, in retrospect, I must have realized that I had penetrated China's veneer of professionalism in a way that I could never achieve with Brittany. I could tell that Brittany was what psycho-analysts would term "very well defended." I knew I could never get truly close to Brittany, but nevertheless I plunged right into her both physically and mentally. We might have succeeded in having sexual intercourse within three minutes of meeting, but rather than leading me toward consummation, the sexuality only heightened my desire to be seduced. Three minutes were like an eternity. I removed her tight blouse, pulling it over her head and unsnapping her bra with a deftness that recalled the great lovers of the European cinema like Mastroianni, Giannini, Léaud, the Belmondo of *Breathless*, and Depardieu. I reached under her tight leather skirt to find nothing and everything at the same time. Even though she was Brittany, she was the kind of Tiffany whose very being released a Pandora's box of emotions and sensations. I was both transported and in control. Was this the mental health I'd been searching for all these years with prostitutes and analysts—a state of heightened desire whose consummation ultimately eluded me?

After we got up from the floor, where we weren't the only couple who had been expressing their uncontrollable passion, and where I'd had a chance to worship the perfection of Brittany's bottom, I found myself following her in a daze like a lost lamb, not even realizing that I had forgotten to zip my fly. My still totally erect penis was jutting out of my pants like a missile about to leave its silo.

I hadn't had a chance to really discover the world of Uva, but as I started getting my bearings again, I realized that the interior was designed to look like the inside of a uterus. I had once seen laparoscopic photos of the inside of the female procreative system, so there was no doubt as to the inspiration for the club's décor, with its pinkish theme interrupted by striations of white. I realized the whole atmosphere was just like a gynecologist's office, where women remove their underwear before climbing into the stirrups for an exam. It was the first time I'd been to a sex club with such a medical theme. If I'd been qualified, which I obviously wasn't, I would have written a paper on it for *The New England Journal of Medicine*. There was even one area that I thought might actually be an on-premise gynecological practice. A woman with her legs spread and raised on something that looked very much like an examination table was attended to by a long line of men who performed cunnilingus on her after they had given her both vaginal and rectal exams, throwing their used rubber gloves in a huge recycling bin when they were finished. It reminded me of the old Mardi Gras Saturday mornings at the Harmony Burlesque in Times Square back in the '70s, when New York was both literally and metaphorically a wide open city. I would have joined the long line of men who were treating Crystal's pudenda as if it were an ice cream cone if I hadn't been so in love with Brittany. My love was actually clouding my ability to take an objective view of my surroundings. What I saw was a succession of sated diners, relaxing together in a huge living room, as the men feasted on pussy and the women seemed to enjoy a spiritual experience that would eventually enable their souls to transcend the limitations of the flesh.

I knew I had to keep my wits about me, but every time I said to myself, *You almost had a fantastic lay and now it's time to get back to your China*, I thought of Brittany's magnificent ass. I wanted to kiss it and hold it. If Brittany had proposed an arrangement whereby she sat on my face indefinitely in exchange for a certain amount of *reality*, I might have agreed. At one point, wandering into one of the more infernal areas of "Les Caves," which reminded me of Manhattan's infamous Hellfire Club, I came across a whole room of men with beautiful Brittanys and Crystals sitting on their faces. These fellows were acting out what I only dreamt of, which was to seek oblivion in the perfect ass of an adored whore. In fact, many of these men looked like wastrels in an opium den, as though they had decided to take a life-altering voyage from which they had little interest in returning. I contemplated the strength of the dollar and wondered how much *reality* it would take to have Brittany sit on my face for the remainder of my stay in Rio. But for the moment, Uva had exceeded my wildest dreams and was far beyond anything I had hoped to find at The Gringo. If it weren't for the ongoing repairs at The Gringo, I never would have discovered Uva, Brittany, and the whole world of renegade Tiffanys who, with their rebellious attitudes and untamed beards, reminded me of the beat poet Allen Ginsberg, although in this case the beards were between their legs. But would I ever be able to extricate myself from the thrall of desire that had overwhelmed me and get back to my dream of building a healthy and loving relationship, either with my China or a real whore?

Reluctantly, I decided it was time to take my leave of Uva. I had no illusion that Brittany would follow me, since I'd lost her long ago as I wandered "Les Caves," where, in addition to face-sitting, vaginal examination, and intercourse, Uva's many patrons were doused with urine, spanked, slapped, placed on the rack, and in one case fucked in the ass by a beautiful Crystal wearing a strap-on. As I came up the cellar steps, emerging from the darkness into the moonlight of the ancient streets, I again encountered the toothless old Charon who had led me to this inferno of desire.

The old man greeted me like a long-lost friend and made it plain that he had been waiting for me and expected compensation for all his efforts on my behalf.

"Where's my thousand dollars?" He spoke the line, which he had undoubtedly lifted from some American gangster film, with an almost perfect Brooklyn accent.

Having paid the wages of sin, I started to walk away. But I questioned why I was even leaving. I had waited this long for pleasure, and now that I'd found it, I wondered if it was simply my childhood fear of asphyxiation that was forcing me to let it slip through my fingers. Nothing was making sense to me, and the prospect of returning to room 1269 to stare into China's vagina while she watched her soccer championships, with the eventual goal of understanding my personality, didn't seem half as enticing as lying in one of Uva's caves with Brittany's beautiful ass in my face. The one similarity with analysis, of course, would be the prone position, although the highly verbal nature of the analytic relationship makes face-smothering counterproductive.

Nevertheless, I began making my way back toward the Copacabana, where some sort of squall seemed to be brewing. The narrow streets gave way to large boulevards, and my obsessive desire turned into a feeling of relief. I had been to hell—a very nice part of hell, but hell nonetheless—and I'd returned to civilization from the infernal regions where sinners burned in the eternity of their unruly desires. Even though I still couldn't shake the conviction that if I weren't so afraid of death I would have given up my last ounce of *reality* to have Brittany sit on my face forever, I was now beginning to get a toehold on my old life of trying to create a real relationship with a prostitute. I couldn't wait to tell China everything that had happened to me, though I was painfully aware that our first session would be over even before I had a chance to get through a fraction of my story. Part of the problem was that I was partial to the slow process of free-associating, abreacting, and describing my dreams. Even in a normal session, by the time I had done all of these things, I would have used up my time. With China, I'd had particular difficulty trying to discuss any of my adventures with the Tiffanys I'd met in Rio. I ended up trying to rehash what I hadn't finished in the previous session, and it could take five or six sessions to get across a minor bit of biography, figuring in the awkward silences with which each session began. At the end of a session, China would inevitably cut me off by saying, "We'll continue next time," at which point I would pause awkwardly to savor a moment of humiliation at being interrupted in the act of expressing an emotion of earth-shattering import. By mutual agreement, I would get up to leave her suite, pause ten seconds, ring the bell, and start it all over again. Having so many sessions in close proximity, we both felt it was best to go through the formality of initiating a new session after a token intermission. It was the cross we had to bear, but it somehow made sense to both of us.

My past analyses were generally slow-going affairs that took place over many years, so the notion that I could have a complete analysis with China in three days, leaving time for the termination process, seemed at first impossible. But I began to look at the analysis with China as one of those life-changing experiences, like climbing Mount Everest or attempting an Iron Man triathlon, in which the human mind is radically altered in a short period of time. Not only would I henceforth look at life totally differently, my view of everything that had happened to me in the past would be shaped by the intense interaction that was taking place as I ogled China's vagina while she shifted in her seat and cheered for her favorite soccer teams. What was essentially going on in the hotel room was a form of shock therapy, in which I came and went so many times that I eventually started to come to grips with my core issue—separation anxiety. Actually, I wasn't totally unfamiliar with the therapeutic approach that China was practicing, since I had once employed it on my dog. Years before, I'd had a basset hound who started to howl every time I left the house. Due to the complaining of my neighbors, I was forced to hire a dog therapist, who diagnosed Hubert's problem as separation anxiety, with the treatment involving the same coming and going that China was applying in my case. Of course, there was more to our analysis than the animal psychology used on my dog. B.F. Skinner notwithstanding, China was plainly interested in behavior modification only to the extent that it helped me to understand the deeper sources of my neurosis.

The true nature of my suffering was a notion that only started to hit me during the latter part of my work with China. During my second day of treatment, after I'd returned from Uva, I started to entertain the notion that China was really only a glorified Tiffany—at least as far as I was concerned. It dawned on me that the only reason I had gone to see her in the first place was to get into her underpants, if she had ever worn any. My whole torrid history started to come back to me—the guilt toward my mother for having worn tight-fitting pants that accentuated my crotch and my general inability to communicate with other human beings, in particular women. I felt like a computer whose hard drive had shut down, and was now coming back to life with distressingly random words, numbers, and images appearing on the screen.

It was early morning and the city was awakening much like my consciousness, which had become short-circuited when my synapses were overheated in Uva. I realized it would soon be time to return to room 1269 to begin what would be the period of the analysis when the patient's transference and the analyst's counter-transference are like two football teams that have ascended to the top of their conferences and are now ready for the Super Bowl. It also reminded me of Hegelian dialectics. If the transference was the thesis, the counter-transference, comprised of the analyst's projections onto the patient, was the antithesis. These two gave birth to a child, or in Hegelian terms, the synthesis, which was the newly psychoanalyzed patient, who had hopefully made his unconscious desires conscious.

I had to shower and freshen up, since my face still smelled of Brittany's ass and I didn't want China to lose her analytic neutrality because of a sudden bout of jealousy, or to say something like, "you smell like shit," which, however truthful, might have hurt my feelings. It would all come out in our sessions, but why put it right in her face, so to speak? There were better ways of communicating my experiences. Normally, I would begin a session by telling my analyst about the dreams I'd had the night before, though in this analysis I had been handicapped by the time structure, which didn't allow for the same kind of elaboration. I was additionally impeded in using this tool of analytic work by the fact that I hadn't slept and could describe no more than my salacious daydreams, which have statistically been found less effective in providing an avenue to the unconscious. As I walked toward the elevator, passing in front of the grand ballroom where the meetings and lectures of the psychoanalytic convention were posted, I noticed that the centerpiece of the day's presentations was "Erotomania: the Sequel," given by Dr. Francesco Levi, from Parma. My curiosity piqued, I continued on my way to China's room.

"I was totally obsessed with Brittany's asshole," I began as soon as I lay back. "There was a moment at Uva when I thought I would do anything to get her back, to have her ass smothering me. At the same time, I wanted to dive into her pussy and swim upstream, as if I could paddle into her uterus and be reborn." As I said this, it dawned on me that even though China was a psychoanalyst, she was also a woman, and I became fearful that she might be offended by the explicitness of the imagery. There was also a bit of dishonesty to my romanticized depiction. I was trying to add a philosophical element, using the dogged quest for rebirth and transcendence as justification for my bawdy fantasies. In truth, I hadn't thought of anything as spiritual as being reborn when I was feasting on Brittany. I was just in love with her ass and the oblivion of unmitigated pleasure it represented. It was as simple as that. I realized I had to be more truthful with China about my feelings if I was ever going to get better.

"Now that I think about it," I continued to ramble, "what is to be found in an asshole or a cunt? I was never satisfied by the attainment of the love object. Once I was licking her ass, I felt strangely bereft. All I was aware of was the mixture of shit and Handy Wipe, like the stench of camphor in a musty closet. Once you gain access to a body part, it loses its symbolic value. Only when it is taken away, as it was when Brittany disappeared into the crowd at the club, does the nimbus that had endowed her organs with otherworldly magic return. I felt like I was in search of the Holy Grail, but now that I am back here in analysis, the feeling is beginning to subside. I'm beginning to realize that Brittany was just a whore. There is something very suspicious about freedom. Nature made breasts, assholes, and cunts to be sacred, and when they are freely exhibited and easily attainable they simply become flesh and bone. There is a certain democratization that goes on at the Copacabana, where the girls walk around topless. After all, the nipple is just calcified skin. The private parts lose their aristocratic quality. The breast, for example, is the child's first sexual object, so it's no wonder that when a grown man finally sees a woman's breast he goes nuts. It's the powerful pull of infantile sexuality in its adult form."

I must say I felt very proud of myself as I finished this little dissertation. I was sure that China would be impressed with the sophistication of my analytic insight, and I was ready and willing to give her credit for having educated me.

"So your mother is just made of skin and flesh and bones like everyone else?" China inquired, raising her eyebrows dispassionately. Somehow her comment reminded me of Shylock's "pound of flesh" in *The Merchant of Venice*, and I imagined my mother taking off her girdle and having her flesh—her breasts, vagina, her stomach—weighed on a scale. I had a sudden urge to get on the next flight back to New York, to leave the Tiffanys and Brittanys of Rio, even to leave my China, and abruptly terminate the analysis. It was apparent that China either hadn't been listening or hadn't understood a word I'd said, because I was making precisely the opposite point: my mother wasn't just skin and bones, any more than China was. It was the way in which the personality infused all this flesh that made a breast more than just a breast. China wasn't just a vagina. Her vagina had symbolic resonance, at least until she had made her brutally insensitive remark. My irritation would soon pass, but for a second I regarded China as no more than a cunt.

She must have been aware of how much her comment upset me, because she dropped her veneer of analytic neutrality and used the remote to lower the volume on her television, despite the fact that she was watching a very important playoff between Brazil and Argentina.

"I think we need to discuss the fee," she said. I felt it was an odd choice to bring up the subject of money when I was in the middle of an emotional discussion about my mother's body. Unfortunately, my time was up. When we began a new session, I immediately explained to China how upset I was with her for discussing fees at a time when I was feeling so fragile. "You're always discussing your mother," she shot back, "even when you think you're not." Then she added, "We'll continue next time." At that moment I felt a rush of contempt for China. I couldn't imagine how we had ever become doctor and patient, much less lovers.

"I hate this Oedipal stuff. It's psychobabble," I blurted. "You know the *Sandinistas*? Well, you sound like a *Jargonista*. It's always the same stuff with loving the mother and hating the father. My father wasn't even in the picture. He was no match for me. It was all about my mother and me. I thought that Lacanians were supposed to be more linguistically orientated. I thought we would be talking about post-structuralists like Barthes, Foucault, and Kristeva. This is the same stale stuff that the classic Freudians were peddling back in the '50s, to go with the Danish modern furniture in the waiting rooms. Sure I loved my mother. Everyone wants to fuck his mother. You don't have to be a patient in psychoanalysis to learn that. I'm actually quite functional. I love women and I simply need to find the right whore to settle down with."

"Do you mind if I suck your cock?" China interjected placidly.

"Sure, but I insist on paying."

China didn't bother to respond as she got down on her knees and started to unzip my fly. When she finally got my dick out, she paused for a moment to listen to a roar from the Brazilian soccer fans on the television, as their goalie made an improbable save. Then she placed me in her mouth.

"You're very eloquent," she said. The words were muffled by the fact that my penis was between her lips, so it would have been dishonest for me to return the compliment. China really knew how to suck a cock, and unlike some Tiffanys she looked you straight in the eye as she did it. Her eyes were actually welling up as she stared at me, as if she were experiencing some powerful emotion.

Perhaps more was happening for her than the simple application of a blowjob. I have to say that I remained curiously rational, despite the oceanic pre-Oedipal feelings that she was stirring up in me. I was painfully aware that my desire was due to the powerful transference that had taken place, and that, like many an analytic patient before me, I had simply fallen in love with my analyst. This is something that is generally more prevalent with women patients, who fall in love with their handsome or fatherly male analysts. But it's perfectly natural for a man to turn his mother figure into a whore. The fact that by blowing my brains out China was giving up her veneer of analytic neutrality complicated matters, but still, all the feelings that were transpiring between us were an inevitable part of the analytic work, and in fact totally appropriate at this stage of the process.

"I just find that you are the most interesting patient I have ever had. You are very special," China said, momentarily ejecting me from her mouth like a DVD. I noted that she was very special too, particularly in regard to her ability to perform psychoanalysis and fellatio at the same time.

"I thought you weren't supposed to say things like that. Every patient always thinks they are special and has a fantasy that the analyst likes him more than all the others."

"But what if I told you that a part of our analysis might be the recognition that you are very special to me, and that I have fallen in love with you."

"But I just want you to be my whore. I want to continue paying you for the sex as well as the analysis."

"I never said you weren't going to pay."

In many ways I was the typical sex tourist. I had come to Rio for the whores, not for love. I'd never even thought of paying for love, but perhaps that was just another way of looking at marriage. You pay a whore for sex and a wife for love. I still had a hunch I was going to be better off paying the whore for sex. Lots of guys I know got married and paid for love, without getting any sex in the bargain.

"I have begun to realize that I have fallen in love with you even if you are my patient," China reiterated. Our session ended just a few seconds later. Normally, I would have been troubled if an analyst dropped such a heavy revelation on me at the end of the session, but in this case all I had to do was walk out of the hotel room, wait ten seconds, then ring the buzzer and come back in.

"Don't you have to work on your counter-transference before you know if you really love me," I began.

"You're using a lot of big words. Why don't you just tell me how you feel?"

That was precisely the problem: my intellectuality is a defense that I often use to avoid confronting my issues. I still play the good student, coming home to mommy and looking for approval. I have always tried to impress my analysts with how much I know about analytic theory. But it's not limited to psychoanalysis. I know just as much about automobile repair as I do about analysis or prostitution. For instance, when I had a problem with the knocking sound coming from the engine of my beat-up, old Ford, I was more knowledgeable about what was going on with the distributor than the mechanic. Like the old comedian

Professor Irwin Corey, I'm one of those guys who tries to be the "world's foremost authority," but sometimes I actually succeed. That was part of the problem. Not only was I gratifying my fantasy of being the best and most interesting patient China had ever had in her practice, I also felt that I could one-up her at her own game. I might not have been able to be a good whore, but I did have the disconcerting feeling that I might have out-analyzed my own analyst. If indeed she had fallen head-over-heels in love with me, as appeared to be the case, I could conceivably be more on top of the situation than she was. Even if I had also fallen for China, I'd been able to maintain my neutrality as a patient. In other words, if she hadn't gotten down on her knees and sucked my cock, I certainly would have been able to curb the turbulent emotions China had aroused in me by exposing the organ that rhymed with her namesake.

"Have you run all this by Schmucker?" I inquired.

"Of course. He's my lover."

A sudden burst of homicidal jealousy served as a good indicator of the depth of my passion for China. While it was considered a breach of professional ethics for an analyst to have sex with his or her patient, there had been many celebrated cases of such goings-on, especially in the early years of analysis, the most famous involving a young woman named Sabina Spielrein, who had been a patient of Jung's.

"He's also your supervisor, isn't he?" I said, thinking that China might consult with Schmucker about me, in the way that Jung had consulted Freud about Spielrein. As I listened to China try to address both my amorous and competitive fantasies, I began to think that someday I might use all the knowledge I'd gained through the painful and joyous experiences of my time in Rio to help other people. I might not become a full-fledged analyst, as Spielrein had, but at the very least I had enough on-site experience to become a counselor to prostitutes.

I'd read about the movement toward intersubjectivity in

analysis, in which the notion of the analyst as a distant tabula rasa on which the patient projects his or her fantasies had been questioned. It was widely acknowledged that the benefits of neutrality are often outweighed by the inequities of a one-sided, at times authoritarian relationship. I wondered if the changing relationship between China and me wasn't reflective of some of the new currents in the psychoanalytic and psychotherapeutic communities. Even though we had only been seeing each other for a relatively short period of time, it was obvious that there was a sea change between our first few minutes together and what was now beginning to transpire. Whether the deeper changes in analytic theory were affecting us or not, there was no doubt that China needed me as much, if not more, than I needed her. One of the by-products of this particular analysis was that the patient and the analyst had reversed roles, with the patient now performing a therapeutic and healing function for his own analyst.

"I think you should probably run this by Schmucker," I suggested.

"I don't think that what has been going on during this session can be called analysis," China confessed. Our session ended, more or less as quickly as it had begun, and when she answered the door after the requisite ten-second interval, her demeanor was markedly changed. She had arranged her blouse and her hair and she seemed remarkably composed. She flipped on the television, as was her custom.

"I don't know where to begin today," I began, pretending that I was a run-of-the-mill analytic patient who came for his 50 minutes once a day, four days a week.

"I feel self-conscious for some reason," I added.

There had never been any pretense about our unconventional schedule at any time during the previous day's sessions. I simply came in and out of the hotel room, neither acknowledging nor denying that it was a strange practice. I just went along with the arrangement, to say nothing of the fact that China often seemed to be more interested in what was on TV than in the analysis itself.

"Why don't you simply talk about your feelings?" she offered.

"I guess what I'm worried about is that I've gotten to like you. You're the kind of whore I could make a life with, but you're my *analyst*. My discomfort is compounded by the fact that I will be returning to New York in a couple of days and I don't even know where your practice is. Of course, you're my analyst, so it's not necessarily important that I know anything more about you other than where I have to go for my appointments. But I feel like it wouldn't be totally unprofessional if you told me a few things about your life in New York. Can we at least make an appointment?"

China looked in her appointment book, which lay on the hassock on which she rested her legs. She had a look of concern on her face. I had to be realistic and confront the fact that it was unlikely she would see me as intensively as she had in Rio. I was afraid that she was going to tell me she couldn't fit me in, but I was flabbergasted when she informed me that, while she had available sessions, she wasn't sure how it would work into my schedule, since she didn't live and practice in New York at all, but in Vancouver.

"Vancouver!" I cried. "I've been telling you I live in Manhattan. Listen, I'd gladly move to Vancouver to marry you and pay you for love, but I'm still trying to find a relationship with a whore I can pay for sex. I guess I was thinking I could get a two-for-one and pay someone to be both my whore and my analyst."

"You feel you are paying for my favors?" she asked, raising one of her perfectly groomed eyebrows.

"Well you wouldn't have seen me unless I'd paid, and I don't think we would have tried to have sex unless we'd had the transference that resulted from the analysis. I've been getting two services for the price of one, and for all intents and purposes I would have been quite satisfied, that is until you informed me that you were geographically challenged."

"Life isn't perfect," China said. She abruptly flicked off the television. The sound of the cheering crowds that had always accompanied our sessions was suddenly gone, and we were just facing each other in silence. I noticed that China's legs were crossed primly in a way that no longer let me see her vagina. Even though she didn't say anything, something had changed between us. Perhaps I'd inadvertently terminated the analysis with my last outburst. Like a good analyst, China had heard what I wasn't yet able to admit to myself. She'd seen that I was beginning to understand the inherent limitations of the analytic situation, and that the person I felt the most intimate with was also someone who wasn't really a part of my life.

I got up and left the room. I could have waited a few seconds and rang the doorbell, pretending nothing had happened, but I didn't. For a moment, standing in the elevator down to the lobby, I wondered if there'd really been an understanding between us, and if the therapy was in fact over.

On a pragmatic level, I also wondered if she was going to charge me for missing our last sessions. I knew in my heart that what I'd seen and felt was true, but, compulsively, I told myself that I ought to go back to room 1269 just to check. I could tell her that I was coming back because I wanted to give her a billing address so she could mail me a final invoice. I would tell her to send the bill to my office, just to make it clear that I wouldn't be coming anymore.

As I walked past the grand ballroom, I noticed that the farewell address of the convention was entitled, "Eros and Agape," and I felt another burst of jealousy and remorse when I saw that the presenter was Herbert Schmucker.

It might defuse the considerable emotional charge left over from our final, dramatic session to come back to her room under the lame pretext of giving her my billing address. But my whole life has been a series of anti-climaxes. Once again, I was making a fool of myself, even if it was for a good cause.

I could just imagine the contempt on China's face when I came slinking back to her room, stammering my tired excuses. If my actions revealed ambivalence about terminating the analysis, they were totally unambiguous in killing any shred of desire she might have had left for me. The elevator was packed with beautiful Tiffanys, all curiously indifferent to me. I would undoubtedly have to deal with this in my next analysis, though at this point I couldn't begin to imagine who I would undertake it with, particularly since I now realized nothing was going to stop me from heading back to her room.

When I finally got my courage up and knocked on China's door, there was no answer. I ran down the corridor, thinking I might find her at the convention. By the time I got to the grand ballroom, there was only a smattering of analysts milling around, and no sign of China, who I assumed had already retired to Schmucker's suite, where no doubt they were passionately embracing in a final lovemaking session before flying home. Beyond the fact that she practiced in Vancouver, I knew almost nothing about China. But Schmucker was a well-known New York psychoanalyst who practiced in Yorkville and had a wife and family. I'd even heard that his children attended Dalton, one of Manhattan's most elite private schools. Any impulse I had to rush up to Schmucker's room to make a final gallant attempt to inform China of my billing address was curbed by a dawning sense of the futility of it all. Perhaps this was what China was trying to demonstrate to me all along, as she watched soccer matches and spread her legs while I poured my heart out to her. My issues with my mother, prostitutes, and tight-fitting jeans were important, but they couldn't compare to the problems that people less fortunate than myself face every day in cities all over the world. Maybe China was trying to give me a little perspective.

I felt a cleansing sadness as I once again walked through the lobby. I'd come across a number of Tiffanys during my stay in Rio, not to mention a Brittany and a China that I was still very attached to. My mind was spinning. I was trying to come to grips with my singular condition, yet I found myself in the middle of a crowded hotel lobby five thousand miles from home trying to inventory my latest tawdry conquests.

I decided to make my way back to the concierge desk where I'd begun my journey. If China had provided me with psycho-analytic insights, the concierges I had dealt with had provided me with therapy of a more practical kind. I had to get back to basics. I'd come to Rio to have sex with Tiffanys, and perhaps what I needed was a Tiffany who was just a good old-fashioned call girl, one who came to my room, did her business, and left. My real problem was the desire to find the perfect whore to settle down with. I didn't need a Tiffany who was the next Anna Freud.

Sometimes the simple pleasures are the best. I hadn't thought about it for a long time, but many men went to prostitutes be-cause they wanted to have sex without the emotional entangle-ments of a relationship. Perhaps I was complicating matters by looking to have a relationship with someone I just wanted to fuck, especially since my intent was simply to enjoy an innocent sex vacation in Rio.

I immediately recognized the attractive woman at the con-cierge desk. I didn't need to be reminded by the silver nameplate on her protuberant chest that it was Suzanne, and I immediately remembered the pledge I had made to myself about asking her if I could purchase the pleasure of her company. Big breasts of-ten create the illusion that they're coming out at you even when they're completely stationary. But everything is a matter of per-ception, and if you choose the quantum view of the universe, which holds that all things are in flux, the Newtonian applecart is easily overturned. As it happened, Suzanne's apples strained the laws of physics, Newtonian or otherwise. Having such enormous breasts was probably a handicap, since most men look at breasts before they notice a face, and I could tell that Suzanne was starved for eye contact.

Roused from the enchantment of her mammaries, I noted the urgency in her voice when she asked if she could be of assistance. I started to hum the words of a Leonard Cohen song: "Suzanne takes you down to her place near the river, you can hear the boats go by, you can spend the night beside her." Suzanne seemed to appreciate my singing because she broke into a smile.

"That's your Leonard Cohen," she said.

"Actually he's Canadian, and I'm American, and I wish your name was Tiffany." I was surprised how quickly I had gotten to the point. Perhaps my lack of inhibition was the result of my analysis with China.

"To be honest, Tiffany is my nickname." Was she hinting at something, or was her nickname really Tiffany? "Well with a name like that you probably need some *reality*."

"I can come to your room in about six hours, when I take my lunch break." That would have been close to dinnertime, but I didn't want to argue with her, considering that Brazilians generally eat lunch when we eat dinner, and dinner when someone like me is having a wet dream.

I agreed to the tryst because of the extraordinary nature of her physical accoutrements, though I realized I still hadn't solved my immediate pleasure problem, and would have to delay gratification unless Suzanne was selfless enough to suggest another Tiffany I could spend time with in the interim. Even though I was very attracted to Suzanne, I'd promised myself that for the rest of my stay in Rio I was going to avoid exclusive attachments. For all of my memorable experiences—my relationship with China, my aristocratic Tiffany, Brittany and her glorious behind, and even the old crone who outfitted me with my first pair of tight jeans—my adventures were beginning to take a toll on me emotionally.

At that moment, I saw Schmucker and China walking out of the elevators that faced the concierge's desk. I quickly finalized my plans to meet Suzanne on her lunch break and snuck away to find a perch where I could observe their interaction.

I was soon disabused of the illusion that I would be able to drown the pain of my separation from China in a series of flings with Suzanne and other beautiful Tiffanys. When Schmucker took China's hand and bent down to kiss her before they walked across the lobby, my heart nearly stopped. I had to contain an urge to confront the two of them about the ethical impropriety of their relationship, but I quickly realized there wasn't anything unethical about two psychoanalysts having a love affair. It may have been painful for me to see them together, but I could hardly say it was improper for the two to have consensual relations. On the other hand, China's dalliances with me were pretty objectionable by even the most lax standards. But, as angry as I was with China, I didn't want to ruin her career. Besides, she could easily have described me as a patient who was ridden with Oedipal feelings of such intensity that they had reached a delusional level.

As the bellboys brought them their luggage, the two analysts looked like colleagues who had simply formed a professional relationship and were now taking leave of each other—knowing they would meet again at a future conference. Perhaps my transference was so powerful that I had made up the intensity of her sexual feelings for Schmucker. Perhaps it was like the scandals involving patients who experience repressed memory syndrome. Perhaps it was just my imagination.

I was faced with a paradox that I think many people in analysis have to contend with. Though my problems seemed small and insignificant compared to those faced by 99% of humanity, they seemed to get more complicated during the course of the treatment. I'd started my work with China feeling mildly confused about the kind of prostitute I wanted to spend the rest of my life with, but by the end of the analysis I had regressed so much that I had murderous Oedipal fantasies about China and her paramour, Schmucker. I suppose this represented progress of sorts. I suppose China might have argued that I was exorcizing the devils that lurked within my psyche. But now, having made the unconscious conscious, where was I?

For starters, I was standing about 100 yards from the electric eye that made the automatic doors of the hotel open and shut. To me, those doors were like the jaws of fate, for beyond them lay the specter of Schmucker and China enacting a parting scene that rivaled that of Lara and Dr. Zhivago. If nothing else, the whole scenario epitomized the disparity between a patient's imagined sense of importance to the analyst and the reality that the analyst has a life of her own.

I knew that I had to turn away from my surrogate parents, China and Schmucker, and find some other whores to play with while I was waiting for Suzanne. The concierge's desk was like a hive for Tiffanys who were working the lobby, but I was feeling hesitant with Suzanne there, despite her distinctly business-like attitude.

I will never underplay the importance of the hotel staff in improving my relations with the Tiffanys of Rio, and I will be forever grateful to the concierge who made sure I was outfitted in trousers that were appropriate for Rio nightlife. Wearing tight crotch-revealing pants is as important in Rio as wearing loose-fitting Brooks Brothers suits if you want to rise in the New York business world. In both cases you have to dress for success. My business attire was as much of an impediment in attracting Tiffanys as tight pants would be if I were looking to build a corporate accountancy clientele in Midtown Manhattan.

I caught the eye of a beautiful and rare Japanese Tiffany. I offered to take her to the hotel's famous sushi bar, but she told me in surprisingly elegant fashion that she already had something nice and fishy I could taste if I wanted to put it in my mouth. Normally I would have been elated, but her suggestion immediately made me think of China, and for a moment I was overcome with a debilitating feeling of grief. However, when she glanced over her shoulder to make sure no one was looking and then picked up her short skirt to show me the goods, I was instantly transported to the fictional hotel room where Holden Caulfield has his first experience with a hooker in *Catcher in the Rye*. This was the only inspiration I needed. After quickly agreeing on a fee, we headed back to my room. She turned out to have a copy of Haruki Murakami's *Kafka on the Shore* in her purse, and was writing her own novel about prostitution called *The Life of a Japanese Geisha in Rio*. She told me the novel was not autobiographical, and reassured me that the notes she was going to take before and after we had sex had nothing to do with me, but were merely renderings of her imaginative life. I noticed that she took notes in English, and when I asked her why she wrote and read in English instead of Japanese, I was stunned by her thoughtful, articulate response.

"That's a good question, Ken. I really think it has to do with the vicissitudes of the publishing industry, particularly in my home country. It is still very hard for a female writer to break into the male-dominated publishing establishment in Japan. It's a little like Lee Krasner playing second fiddle to Jackson Pollock. I'm also practicing my English so I can get more American customers who don't skimp on *reality*. I'm saving up so that I can come to the States. My great dream is to be a whore and writer in New York. You know, *Breakfast at Tiffany's* was really a novel about prostitution. I bet you didn't know that Audrey Hepburn was actually a well-known streetwalker before she became an actress. Lots of prominent women were once hookers: Eleanor Roosevelt, Marie Curie, even Martha Washington. At least that's what they taught us when I was growing up in Japan."

Were it not for the lack of underwear and the leather micro-skirt that failed to hide her wisp of jet-black pubic hair, Tiffany would have looked like one of the geishas she was writing about, with her doll-like features, her demure composure, and the heavy white pancake makeup she wore on her face. She had the look of one of the actresses in a traditional theater performance I attended on a trip to Japan during my junior year in college. I was more than ready for this kind of exotica, but for a Tiffany to provide me with the attentions administered by a typical geisha could take longer than a staging of a classic Noh drama. Ironically, Tiffany turned out to be more interested in sex than I was, particularly since I was hoping to save some of my vital fluids for my assignation with Suzanne. Alas, since her primary motivation was to make money as quickly as possible to finance her immigration to the United States, this Noh-drama Tiffany showed little interest in any drawn-out sexual theatrics. I couldn't bear the sadness that came over her face when she realized that she was going to have to spend more time on preliminaries than she had reckoned on. I finally caved and let her take her clothes off and give me a quick blowjob, if only to make her feel like a productive member of Rio's sex-worker community—with the proviso that I didn't want her to be offended if I refused to come.

I ended up with a case of blue balls that was only palliated by the taste left in my mouth after sampling her delicacies, which eclipsed the finest sashimi served at New York's famed Nobu. I gave her a good dose of *reality* before sending her off to pursue her publishing dreams, but I still had some time to kill. I turned on the television to one of the local educational channels, which featured a program with English subtitles about whether or not the Virgin Mary was a virgin, using some stains on a burial shroud to argue its point.

Having enjoyed a late-afternoon snack, I fell into a comfortable snooze. By the time I woke up, it was almost time to see

Suzanne. I had given her my room number, so all I really had to do was wait in bed for her, but I realized it might be best to hop in the shower to wash away any residual smells. After rinsing off, I decided to wander down to the lobby, which was beginning to resonate with all kinds of nostalgic associations, even though I'd only been staying in Rio for the better part of a week. I felt a little like the aging professor in Bergman's *Wild Strawberries*, who reminisces about his past life and loves. I walked through the lobby and out onto the Copacabana, enjoying the spectacle of a beautiful beach packed with whores. As I sauntered back into the lobby, I noticed that Suzanne was no longer behind the concierge's desk and understood that the moment had come for me to savor the pleasures of what I imagined to be one of the finest whores Rio had to offer. Life was becoming almost poetic in its simplicity. All it would take was a good dose of *reality* and I would be on my way. After that, I would fly back to New York, to another kind of reality—the reality of my life.

Perhaps I had been lulled into complacency. I thought I would simply return to my room to find Suzanne the sex kitten waiting for me under the sheets, but that didn't exactly happen. I did go back to my room, and even rang the bell on the off chance she had let herself in and was in the process of douching in preparation for my arrival. But she wasn't there. I started to worry that perhaps she'd already come and gone. She might even put a charge on my hotel bill for missing an appointment without prior notice. I had seen my share of Tiffanys during my stay in Rio, but I was disconsolate to miss out on Suzanne's services. I felt a little like an alpinist who's spent months preparing for an ascent, only to have the expedition called off due to bad weather. Suzanne possessed the only mountain range I really wanted to climb, and I was so frustrated that I was on the verge of going into the bathroom to jerk off when all of a sudden there was a ring at the door.

In astronomy, there is a phenomenon called syzygy, which

occurs when the sun, moon, and earth are all in alignment. As Suzanne walked through the threshold of my suite, throwing her shoulder bag down on one of the plush loveseats, her nameplate popping spontaneously off her chest, I knew some kind of cosmic synchronicity had taken hold. She didn't even ask for a dose of *reality*, so intent was she on her transformation into Tiffany. She unbuttoned the blouse of her uniform to reveal perhaps the sexiest bra I had ever seen on a whore. To describe it as a mere black French bra with delicate lace fringe does not do it proper justice. It was a bra for a woman whose breasts have long since declared their independence from support of any kind, as India did in 1948. That is to say, it was a bra in name only. Rather, it was a monumental allusion to that point in the history of feminine attire when breasts were accorded a new kind of opening curtain—one that came off rather than going up at the beginning of an act.

Like a hypnotist snapping her fingers to bring me out of my trance, Suzanne told me to unhook her peerless brassiere. My hands trembled as I circled her nervously, as transfixed by the dorsal view of her nakedness, the arch and small of her back, as I was by the prospect of laying my eyes on her breasts, which were now just a glimmer, albeit a colossal one, in my imagination, a vision beyond the grasp of my engorged senses.

Adam and Eve covered themselves for a reason. It was not simply the temptation of sin that brought shame. It was the recognition that the advent of consciousness necessitated an added bit of showmanship in the sexual act. The hoopla accorded to the covering of the genitals, especially for women, was in fact naturally selective. It was what gave sexuality its mystery and encouraged procreation. Only the conceit of a great metaphysical love poem, like Andrew Marvell's "To His Coy Mistress," could capture the mind-body chasm that was bridged as I feasted my eyes on Suzanne's perfection.

I was willing to pay anything to have sex with Suzanne. The

fact that I could blow caution to the wind and max out my credit card was part of the thrill. When I am in the presence of a delicious, half-undressed Tiffany like Suzanne, I am like a gambler at the high stakes table in Las Vegas. I was ready to throw in my chips and go all-or-nothing.

Suzanne quickly wriggled out of her skirt and panties. In all my years of visiting whores, I had never seen secondary sex characteristics like the ones I now witnessed. Her areolae were soft and golden brown and her nipples stood at attention like they were singing the Marseillaise. The breasts themselves recalled the words of another metaphysical poet, John Donne, who had said about one woman's body, "Oh my America, my new found land." Suzanne's tits had cosmological significance. They were like the most beautiful celestial body, like Venus spied through a telescope as it orbits in space. But this was no comparison to what lay below. Looking between Suzanne's legs reminded me of visiting the famous garden created by Vita Sackville-West at Sissinghurst. I had seen some dramatic landscaping the last time I was in England, but nothing compared to the resplendent nature, the shooting tangle of dark growth, the topiary, the great looming hedge that festooned the smoldering estate that lurked between Suzanne's thighs.

"Tiffany, before we make love, I just wanted to settle up," I gasped. "That way we can enjoy ourselves without having to think about money." Despite my romantic feelings toward most Tiffanys, and my willingness to pay anything for a woman I loved, I also have a pragmatic side.

"My nickname's not really Tiffany," Suzanne corrected me. Was I hearing correctly or was she just teasing? "I don't have a whore name. I was kidding. I just really love sex."

I could hardly breathe. It was Cinderella in reverse. The beautiful princess turned into an old crone before my eyes. The thought that she wasn't a prostitute and that I didn't have to pay for sex was so repugnant to me that I lost all interest in her. I prayed that there was some sort of misunderstanding, but in the meantime the erection I'd been massaging contentedly ever since she took off her top immediately faded. My penis wilted like a rotted carrot, seeming to disintegrate between my fingers. I knew there was no way I was going to get it back up. All I could think of was how to get rid of her. You can just give a common whore a dose of *reality*, tell her you don't feel like it, and send her on her way. But the average woman doesn't like it when she comes to your room and reveals her naked body only to be told you're no longer interested. As I was to find out, Brazilians are a particularly passionate lot who don't tolerate rejection well.

"Since you're not a Tiffany, I am no longer interested," I sniffed. I decided that to compensate for the language barrier I should be as emphatic as possible. Suzanne might as well have been a man. That's how little attraction I had for a woman who wasn't a whore.

Suzanne pleaded with me, saying, "I'm as good as a whore. I'll sleep with almost anybody. Isn't that enough?" But her pleading soon turned into insistent demands. I had learned the difference between a request and a demand in therapy, and I tried to communicate this distinction to her, but it was already too late. She wouldn't listen to reason. When I made it emphatically clear that I had no intention of fucking her, she quickly got dressed, slapped me across the face, and cried out, "I never met such a pig in my whole life," before slamming the door behind her. If she had been a man, and we had been in 19th-century Russia, her behavior might have resulted in a duel. Instead, I was simply left in my room trying to figure out what I was going to do with the rest of my evening, particularly since I had no intention of going down to the concierge's desk and running the risk of encountering the enraged Suzanne.

I tend to feel guilty even when I haven't done anything wrong. It's something I've long dealt with in analysis, particularly with regards to my attitude toward women. I know there are people who feel that it's wrong for a woman to sell her body, and that men who pay for sex are complicit in a crime both against women and society. I can be made to endorse someone's worldview if they are forceful enough in their opinions. To me, the critic has a certain authority, while the person who praises and supports is merely a flatterer. I can go to a party filled with happy, contented whores who are glad to see me and eager to sell their bodies for sex, but end up obsessing about the one radical feminist who shows her opposition to prostitution by refusing to talk to me. But I had to stick to my guns before it was too late. I realized that although my stay in Rio was coming to an end, I had a right, nay an obligation, to run out and find a real Tiffany to take Suzanne's place. Feeling vulnerable, I decided to put my jeans back on, despite how shapeless they'd become, and head back downstairs.

The sublime experience of talking about my Oedipal feelings toward my mother while staring up China's twat reconfirmed my notion that the best things in life aren't free. There are certain experiences you are only going to have if you are willing to pay for them. My problems with Suzanne's sexual altruism, which had dulled my interest in sex for all of five minutes, made me think that there might be other things besides women and psychoanalysis that are worth paying for. One of them was friendship. I'd always had trouble making friends because of my control issues, but I realized that buying friendship might be one way to stay in control. It was like buying shares in a company. If you had a controlling interest, you were able to influence the decision-making process. However, being just another shareholder was no fun, unless of course the company was reporting quarterly gains and had a significant price-earnings ratio.

As these thoughts streamed through my mind, my eyes alighted on what I thought was an apparition. I blinked several times to make sure my vision wasn't blurred. Sure enough, it was my old pal John Joneszzzz, a severely delayed kid I had hung out with in elementary school. John was one of those kids who made up with willpower what he lacked in brains. I always knew he was going places, and I was right—here he was in Rio. John Jones is a very common name, so his parents, wanting to add some excitement to his life, had added the z's, naming him after a comic book character who was a little different because he was from outer space. While legend had it that Schmucker had been one of the smartest kids in Yorkville, graduating from PS 6 and going on to do what most super-smart kids did in those days, which is to become a high priced psychoanalyst, Joneszzzz went into real estate sales, which is what all the dumb kids did.

He went on to make more money selling condos during the gentrification of his old Yorkville neighborhood than the stuck-up Schmucker would see in a lifetime of dozing while his patients complained about their miserable childhoods.

"Hey, old buddy! You haven't changed a bit," I said, as I girded myself for his simian embrace. It was the same old enthusiastic John. I was sure he would displace one of my vertebrae as he clamped me in his vice-like arms. He had piercing blue eyes and a face as flat as a frying pan. "Great to see you, bud," I wheezed, as he nearly squeezed the life out of me.

"The name's John. John Joneszzzz with four z's!" he hollered jovially. John was still a little slow.

"How could I ever forget John Joneszzzz with four z's! I meant *bud* as an endearment."

"A what? You always did use big words. I heard you went to Columbia. They use a lot of big words up there I bet."

"Forget it. It's just great to see you. How long are you here for?"

"I don't know. My wife takes care of that kind of stuff." John was always a happy-go-lucky guy who didn't bother with anything he couldn't understand, which was just about everything.

John's wife was a breed apart from the girls who wandered along the Copa in string bikinis. She was walking through the lobby of the hotel with a kerchief around her head and her hair still in curlers, in a style still popular in certain parts of Yorkville.

"John, where the hell have you been?" she bellowed. "You were supposed to pick the kids up by the pool at five so I could get my nails done!" She didn't pay any attention to me, and she didn't seem to care that her husband had run into an old friend in the middle of Rio. John tried to interrupt her to explain the chance circumstances of our encounter, but she refused to listen. As she dragged him away by the sleeve, he whispered, "Have you seen any of the hookers?"

I felt that getting John a hooker was the least I could do. It was like sending a care package to Myanmar. Considering the irrational phobia I had developed about the concierge's desk, and the fact that John's wife would likely watch over him vigilantly, I had my work cut out for me. But my grandfather, an immigrant who had fled the pogroms in Russia and made his way to America by way of South Africa when he was only 14, always said, "Where there's a *vill*, there's a *vay*!" Those words have never left me, even in the most difficult situations I've confronted in life. I decided to go down to the Copa. Once I had located the merchandise, I would come back to the lobby, call up to John Joneszzzz's room, and tell him there was a little business venture I needed to discuss with him. When he came down, I would hand over the girl and my own room key. I felt strongly that as alumni of PS 6, we needed to stick together, and I was actually feeling bad for the fact that Joneszzzz was pussy-whipped by his petty tyrant of a wife, despite all his hard work and success.

My own will was flagging because of the incident with Suzanne, and I was beginning to consider going home early. All in all, I'd had an active vacation. I'd seen Rio and had gotten to know some of its people. Rio had more than lived up to its reputation, and I wasn't the least bit disappointed. But I started to think that despite the chain of events that led to Suzanne storming out of my room and calling me a pig, I wanted to leave on a positive note, preserving at least my good memories of The Catwalk, Uva, and my first sessions with China, which had left an indelible impression on me.

I succeeded in getting Joneszzzz set up with a real floozie. This Tiffany even had *puta*, the Portuguese word for whore, tattooed on her back, in case anyone needed to identify the item they were purchasing. Like the medieval scholastics, who weighed questions like how many angels can stand on the head of a pin, I often find myself adjudicating ridiculous questions. So I asked myself, if I wanted to import a Tiffany like the one I had purchased for Joneszzzz, would I have to declare her at customs, like a watch or a piece of jewelry? As I gnawed idly on this intellectual cud, it struck me that I had completely lost touch with *reality*, both in the literal and figurative senses of the word. If I kept buying expensive hookers, I was going to go broke. I had a nice accountancy practice, but most of my net worth was invested in hedge funds, which had been experiencing some alarming fluctuations in value. You can invest and hope for the best, but no matter how big a commission or advisory fee you pay, there is no way of predicting whether the market is heading up or plunging into a nose-dive. Money could buy sex, and even love, but money itself offered no guarantees for its own future. Yet seeing the look of gratitude on Joneszzzz's face when he emerged from the elevator and returned my room key after a good lay would have been worth all of my money, or at the very least a million dollars.

Joneszzzz turned out to be even more grateful for my generosity than I could have ever expected. "Just between you and me, I haven't been able to get it up with my old lady lately," he said, shaking my hand in his enthusiastic, salesman-like way. "Now I feel like a man again." He actually puffed out his chest in such a way that for a moment he looked like Popeye. After meeting his wife, I wasn't surprised he couldn't get it up. Her personality alone could have wilted a titanium dildo.

"If you ever need a condo in Yorkville, lemme know. I'm known as the Condo King," he said as he left, then leaned in to whisper, "It's a license to print money, believe me. But you don't look like you're doing so bad yourself. Hey, I like those jeans. Don't show them to your mother."

For a moment I considered Joneszzzz's offer of a Yorkville condo. I'd heard that elegant Tiffanys regularly frequented the East Side high-rises, and that most of the new buildings had health clubs that were filled with whores. My Upper West Side building, with its clanging radiators, was filled with old Jewish widows who tenaciously held onto the rent-controlled apartments they had occupied for millennia. Of course, a few of these Yiddishe mamas had been Tiffanys when they were young. You find Tiffanys in all walks of life. For instance, I heard that one of the librarians at my local public library, a scholarly-looking young lady who talked softy and wore bifocals, gave hand jobs behind the checkout desk on Saturday afternoons.

However, I preferred the idea of going home to a place that was close to my intellectual roots. I was only blocks from my alma mater and from the world of Isaac Bashevis Singer (another great whoremonger), Hannah Arendt (Martin Heidegger's whore), and the spawning ground of the *Partisan Review* and the other great intellectual journals of the '50s, with their coteries of whoremongers (Edmund Wilson) and sluts (Mary McCarthy). I could also hop on the Broadway local, change at 72nd Street and find myself with a scholarly prostitute in a matter of minutes.

I'd succeeded in getting what I had come for, and would return home to New York while I was still ahead of the game. Rio had been as close as I'd ever come to paradise. It wasn't only the high quality of the whores and the fact that they were so easy to find (especially after I improved my wardrobe), it was also the quality of the therapy. Obviously, there was a lot to say about China, but I couldn't fault her for the excellent quality of her analytic work and the freshness of her insights. I had a feeling there were lots of good analysts in Rio—perhaps as many analysts hung out their shingles as whores. I'd already booked my following year's vacation in Bangkok, and the year after that I was planning to attend the international convention of sex workers, which is held biannually in Amsterdam. I've been to those meetings before, and many of the presentations are quite enlightening in describing the prospects for prostitution in the twenty-first century.

Some people go to see the Taj Mahal, or the other six wonders of the world, but I'm a committed sex tourist who never tires of seeing beautiful Tiffanys in exotic locales. Over the years, I've heard many articulate, well-educated prostitutes speak about their trade. They are autodidacts accustomed to self-stimulation (they prefer mental masturbation when they are not working), and their presentations are well informed, with a mixture of practical experience and theory. I'll never forget one lecture I heard, entitled "How Much is That Doggy in the Window: the Role of the Prostitute in the Free Market Economy." It was written by a full professor of economics at the University of California at Berkeley whose supply-side analysis of prostitution was based on her own experiences as a streetwalker in San Francisco's Tenderloin.

I got my courage up and went to the concierge's desk, which was now staffed by a fabulous-looking young woman whose badge identified her as Martine. I might have been tempted to arrange one last fling if I hadn't noticed the prominent Adam's apple that was a dead give-away of her true gender. Some transsexuals talk freely about their operations, and for a moment I toyed with the notion of asking her if she had gotten her vagina yet or if she was still a pre-op transvestite with a pair of breasts. It's easy enough to get breasts, but it's the vagina that's complicated and expensive. I could have been just another tourist asking a guide about the Pyramids or the Parthenon, but I put my curiosity on the back burner so that I could change my flight arrangements.

Martine spoke softly but had the voice of a tenor. Our eyes met as she looked up from the schedule of flights she was studying on her computer screen, and I could almost see her thinking, "Yes, in answer to your question, Mr. Cantor, I still have a penis." Instead, she said politely, "Okay, Mr. Cantor, with your kind of ticket I have no seats for the direct flight back to New York, but there is room on a flight to Miami early tomorrow morning, with a connecting flight to New York that gets you home by early evening." I had an immediate desire to inquire about Suzanne, as if Suzanne and I were long-lost lovers and Martine was the go-between who would tell me how she was faring and what kind of life she was leading after our breakup. I guess this was just my way of dealing with my lingering upset about Suzanne calling me a pig. I could easily have bonded with Martine about Suzanne's unjustified cruelty, but I have learned to practice restraint in foreign countries, where there are all kinds of powerful underworld gangs, religious fanatics, and sometimes even arcane laws against slander. I didn't want to start up any kind of vendetta against Suzanne that might have resulted in a price being put on my head.

I could tell that Martine was beginning to have feelings for me, which I knew I wouldn't be able to reciprocate. I quickly agreed to the flight change and decided to go out onto the Copa and take the first halfway decent-looking hooker I came across back to my room. Horniness is like hunger. It can catch up with you quite suddenly if you miss a meal. With all the turmoil over Suzanne and the excitement of running into John Joneszzzz, I had neglected my own needs. By the time I got to the beach I was overcome with an insatiable urge. But I had to exercise restraint for fear of stumbling into another debacle with a woman who refused to take money for sex.

I was back to where I started. Several Tiffanys in tiny string bikinis passed by, negotiating the sandy beach in their stiletto heels. "Pssst… show me your vagina," I hissed, recalling the most tried and true methods of seduction. One of them turned back and nonchalantly pointed her finger at her cunt, whose labia were visible beneath the thin material of her bikini. As I soon found out, this Tiffany's name was Marguerita. She accompanied me back to my room for a quick fuck. After she was done, she even helped me pack when I told her I was leaving the next morning. It wasn't the best sex I'd ever had, nor was Marguerita affiliated with any of the Brazilian psychoanalytic institutes. However, when it was over I realized it was the one time I had successfully consummated the act of sexual intercourse during my whole odyssey in Rio. Was it Eliot who famously said, "not with a bang but a whimper"?

Tiffany could tell I had been through the wringer, and she would have made herself available for a little chat, since the deed itself had been accomplished in a relatively short space of time. Brazilian hookers, unlike their American counterparts, are not clock-watchers. But it would have taken some time to go into everything, and I wanted to conserve my remaining *reality* so I could buy something for my mother at the airport's duty-free shop.

After Marguerita left, I opened the shades and looked out at all the scantily clad Tiffanys on the beach. The sky was clear, but for the first time during my vacation I noticed large gray clouds looming on the horizon. I don't know if I was projecting, but those clouds reminded me of China. There was something about the cumulus formations that evoked her Asian ancestry, combined with her fearsome ability to kick up a storm. I felt a twinge of love and affection for her, combined with irritation at the way she had abused her authority. She was very proud and I knew she would never recant, but I wondered if her talents might not be put to better use if she became a hooker who listened to her clients' problems rather than a therapist who fucked her patients. My eyelids were getting heavy, and as I dozed off I began seeing my whole vacation in Rio play out before my eyes, like I was having a near-death experience. I fell into a deep sleep, and if it hadn't been for the wake-up call from the concierge's desk, I might have missed my flight.

Shaken from the depths of my slumber, I groped for the phone. I immediately recognized the voice at the other end. "Suzanne, is that you?" I cried. But before I had a chance to say anything else, she hung up. For a moment I entertained the thought that she might be coming back up to the room to finish what she had started, maybe even pretending to be a whore and consenting to take some money just to consummate the act. But no such luck. Suzanne would not be making an appearance. Perhaps I'd experienced a moment of temporary insanity and she hadn't called at all.

The trip to the airport was uneventful. The road leading to the main terminal was lined with Tiffanys who raised their skirts and blouses to display their goods, but I was a hardened sex tourist, and the sight of hookers showing off their wares was no different than looking at the Arche de Triomphe or any other stale tourist attraction. I was looking forward to getting home.

Besides exploring China's pussy, I hadn't done any real analytic work for some time, and I knew that the trip to Rio would be real grist for the mill. I was even toying with the idea of calling China in Vancouver to see if she could refer me to one of her colleagues in New York, since she already knew so much about my case. I didn't pause for a moment when I went through customs and the inspector asked me if I had purchased any goods in the country. I certainly had, but I figured in this case discretion was the better part of valor. If I told the truth and said I had purchased many girls, I might be mistaken for a slave trader and wind up missing my flight.

I was originally assigned a cramped seat in the middle of my row, but the attractive Brazilian woman sitting at my side batted her eyelashes at me flirtatiously as she relinquished her aisle seat. She was obviously a whore, and probably figured the deferential treatment might make the trip pay off. After lift-off the stewardess came around to take drink orders. She was tall, dark, and attractive, her skirt provocatively short. When she bent down to ask me what I would like, I noticed the gold nameplate on the breast pocket of her blouse. "Tiffany," it read.

ACKNOWLEDGEMENTS

I wish to thank Adam Ludwig for his editorial guidance. Adam is like a pilot coolly navigating turbulence with acute intelligence, patience and a recognition of the imminence of disaster. I would also like to thank Eric and Eliza Obenauf. Getting published by Two Dollar Radio is a cutting edge experience. I learned about Mark Danielewski's *House of Leaves* from reading Eric's blog and I look forward to finishing it before the copyright for *Seven Days in Rio* runs out. With regard to commas, suffice it to say that Eliza doesn't agree with those who argue, "if in doubt leave it out." I can't exactly thank my wife Hallie Cohen for our endless "discussions" about writing. I would like to take this opportunity to tell her that it's not so bad to use an object instead of a subject pronoun.

ALSO BY FRANCIS LEVY

EROTOMANIA: A ROMANCE

A NOVEL

A Trade Paperback Original; 978-0-9763895-7-6; $14 US

* *Inland Empire Weekly* Standout Book of 2008.
* *Queerty* Top 10 Book of 2008.

"Sex is familiar, but it's perennial, and Levy makes it fresh." —Richard Rayner, *Los Angeles Times*

"[A] hilariously satirical debut novel. Miller, Lawrence, and Genet stop by like proud ancestors." —Zach Baron, *The Village Voice*

A COMEDIC, ABSURDIST PORTRAIT OF A MODERN-DAY ROMANCE, *Erotomania* traces the development of James and Monica, from a couple that is forced to move to a nuclear fall-out bunker so their explosive sex life doesn't physically harm their neighbors, to James' one-night bout with alcoholism, to Monica's sexually-fueled obsession with abstractionist expressionism, to marriage counseling, to a new-found reliance on reality television and microwaveable meals.

THE VISITING SUIT

A NOVEL BY XIAODA XIAO

A Trade Paperback Original; 978-0-9820151-7-9; $16.50 US

"[Xiao] recount[s] his struggle in sometimes unexpectedly lovely detail. Against great odds, in the grimmest of settings, he manages to find good in the darkness." —Lori Soderlind, *New York Times Book Review*

THE CAVE MAN

A NOVEL BY XIAODA XIAO

A Trade Paperback Original; 978-0-9820151-3-1; $15.50 US

* *WOSU* (NPR member station) Favorite Book of 2009.

"As a parable of modern China, [*The Cave Man*] is chilling." —*Boston Globe*

THE ORANGE EATS CREEPS
A NOVEL BY GRACE KRILANOVICH
A Trade Paperback Original; 978-0-9820151-8-6; $16 US
* National Book Foundation 2010 '5 Under 35' Selection.
* *NPR* Best Books of 2010.
* *The Believer* Book Award Finalist.

"Krilanovich's work will make you believe that new ways of storytelling are still emerging from the margins." —*NPR*

TERMITE PARADE
A NOVEL BY JOSHUA MOHR
A Trade Paperback Original; 978-0-9820151-6-2; $16 US
* *Sacramento Bee* Best Read of 2010.

"[A] wry and unnerving story of bad love gone rotten. [Mohr] has a generous understanding of his characters, whom he describes with an intelligence and sensitivity that pulls you in. This is no small achievement." —*New York Times Book Review*

SOME THINGS THAT MEANT
THE WORLD TO ME
A NOVEL BY JOSHUA MOHR
A Trade Paperback Original; 978-0-9820151-1-7; $15.50 US
* *O, The Oprah Magazine* '10 Terrific Reads of 2009.'

"Charles Bukowski fans will dig the grit in this seedy novel, a poetic rendering of postmodern San Francisco."
—*O, The Oprah Magazine*

THE PEOPLE WHO WATCHED HER PASS BY
A NOVEL BY SCOTT BRADFIELD
A Trade Paperback Original; 978-0-9820151-5-5; $14.50 US

"Challenging [and] original... A billowy adventure of a book. In a book that supplies few answers, Bradfield's lavish eloquence is the presiding constant."
—*New York Times Book Review*

1940

A NOVEL BY JAY NEUGEBOREN
A Trade Paperback Original; 978-0-9763895-6-9; $15 US
   * Long list, 2010 International IMPAC Dublin Literary
     Award.

"Jay Neugeboren traverses the Hitlerian tightrope with all the
skill and formal daring that have made him one of our most
honored writers of literary fiction and masterful nonfiction."
—Tim Rutten, *Los Angeles Times*

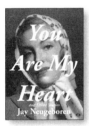

YOU ARE MY HEART AND OTHER STORIES

STORIES BY JAY NEUGEBOREN
A Trade Paperback Original; 978-0-9826848-8-7; $16 US

"[Neugeboren] might not be as famous as some of his
compeers, like Philip Roth or John Updike, but it's becoming
increasingly harder to argue that he's any less talented...
dazzlingly smart and deeply felt."
—Michael Schaub, *Kirkus Reviews*

THE CORRESPONDENCE ARTIST

A NOVEL BY BARBARA BROWNING
A Trade Paperback Original; 978-0-9820151-9-3; $16 US

"This novel of an affair told prismatically is a love letter to
letters, a passionate mixtape to the world of culture."
—Kevin Thomas, *The Rumpus*

"A deft look at modern romance that is both witty and
devastating." —*Nylon*

I SMILE BACK

A NOVEL BY AMY KOPPELMAN
A Trade Paperback Original; 978-0-9763895-9-0; $15.00 US

"Powerful. Koppelman's instincts help her navigate these
choppy waters with inventiveness and integrity."
—Paul Kolsby, *Los Angeles Times*

Also published by **TWO DOLLAR RADIO**

THE SHANGHAI GESTURE
A NOVEL BY GARY INDIANA
A Trade Paperback Original; 978-0-9820151-0-0; $15.50 US

"An uproarious, confounding, turbocharged fantasia that manages, alongside all its imaginative bravura, to hold up to our globalized epoch the fun-house mirror it deserves."
—*Bookforum*

THE DROP EDGE OF YONDER
A NOVEL BY RUDOLPH WURLITZER
A Trade Paperback Original; 978-0-9763895-5-2; $15.00 US
* *Time Out New York*'s Best Book of 2008.
* *ForeWord* Magazine 2008 Gold Medal in Literary Fiction.

"A picaresque American *Book of the Dead*... in the tradition of Thomas Pynchon, Joseph Heller, Kurt Vonnegut, and Terry Southern." —*Los Angeles Times*

NOG
A NOVEL BY RUDOLPH WURLITZER
Trade Paperback; 978-0-9820151-2-4; $15.50 US

"A strange, singular book... somewhere between Psychedelic Superman and Samuel Beckett." —*Newsweek*

"The Novel of Bullshit is dead." —Thomas Pynchon

"Nog is to literature what Dylan is to lyrics."
—Jack Newfield, *The Village Voice*

FLATS / QUAKE
TWO NOVELS BY RUDOLPH WURLITZER
Trade Paperback; 978-0-9820151-4-8; $17 US

Two countercultural classics from Rudolph Wurlitzer now available in one "69ed" edition.

"Wurlitzer might be the closest thing we have to an actual cult author, a highly talented fiction writer."
—*Barnes & Noble Review*